NEW YEAR'S WITH THE SINGLE DAD

SINGLE DADS OF SEATTLE, BOOK 6

WHITLEY COX

ISBN: 978-1-989081-25-9

For Danielle and Jillian,
my critique partners and two seriously awesome bitches.
Thank you for everything.

1

COFFEE!

He needed coffee.

He needed to hook himself up to an espresso IV or at the very least put his large black coffee into a camel pack on his back.

How in the world was he going to get through this day? This night?

Stomping off the snow from his black dress shoes and loosening the collar of his coat, Dr. Emmett Strong stepped toward the front counter of the downtown Seattle coffee shop. What were the odds he'd managed to arrive at just the right moment and miss standing in line for twenty minutes?

Were things finally looking up?

It was about time.

He walked up to one of the two baristas standing there, waiting to take orders.

"What can I getcha?" the barista with the goatee asked him, his red tie just slightly crooked.

"Large coffee with two shots of espresso, please. And an everything bagel toasted with cream cheese, lox and cucumber slices." His brow instantly furrowed as he heard his order come out of his mouth and realized it was somehow said in stereo.

The two baristas behind the counter at the side-by-side cash registers gave him and the person next to him an equally surprised, almost spooked look. They had apparently ordered the exact same thing at the exact same time.

What were the odds?

He turned to see who shared his taste in breakfasts to find a very attractive woman laughing. Her light brown hair was cut in a sleek bob that fell just beneath her chin, and her sky-blue eyes sparkled.

"Good choice," she said, continuing to laugh. "Just know that if they only have one bagel left, it's got my name on it. I'm running late for work, and I'm freaking starved."

"You two don't know each other?" the male barista asked.

Emmett shook his head. So did the striking woman beside him.

"Just kindred breakfast spirits," she said lightly.

"We have enough bagels for both," the female barista said, her chipper tone indicating she'd probably had a shot or two—or three—of espresso herself that morning. "Though we've never had the exact same order at the exact same time like that. It was spooky."

The two baristas continued to ring up Emmett and this mystery woman's breakfast. They both pulled out credit cards and paid, then moved to the side like well-trained cattle so the next hungry Seattle caffeine addict could pump ethically traded Arabica into their bloodstream and make it through the day—and what was inevitably going to be a long night for everyone.

Even though it was now New Year's Eve day, Christmas decorations still hung from the ceiling and painted the coffee shop windows, and the radio station over the speakers continued to blast out tunes like Mariah Carey's "All I Want for Christmas." He would be glad when they could get back to the regular scheduled programming of tasteful classic rock and no sparkly shit hitting his head as he waited for his breakfast.

Until Valentine's season hit them like that fat winged-baby's arrow, that is. Then it'd be all red and pink hearts and more glitter—AKA the herpes of craft supplies. His almost six-year-old daughter, JoJo, loved anything and everything sparkly. He was always finding glitter in the laundry, his shoes—his food.

She needed to keep that crap at her mother's.

He glanced at the woman beside him. She was tall. Not super tall, not taller than his six-three frame, but taller than his ex. Taller than most women.

She held her chin up with a confidence he admired, her eyes laser-focused forward, her full lips resting in a kind line. She had a great profile, and an air of ease and sureness surrounded her like a soft glow.

He must have been staring too intensely because her eyes slid to the side and she turned to face him. "Think they'll put the orders up at the same time, or are we going to have to duke it out for the first one?"

Emmett's lip twitched into a small smile. "You can have it."

Her light blue eyes squinted just slightly, and she made a fist with her hand and flexed her coat-covered arm. "You sure you don't want to arm-wrestle for it?"

Emmett chuckled and scanned the coffee shop. "Afraid there are no empty tables." He snapped his fingers. "Shucks. And I was *so* looking forward to kicking your butt."

He'd been in a crappy mood this morning—too much beer at poker night last night—combined with the fact this past year had been complete shit. But this woman's smile pulled him from the dark place he'd woken up in. In fact, her wide smile made his stomach do a somersault and caused heat to pool in various places in his body—various *intimate* places.

"Oh, that's some ego you got there," she said, her carefree attitude causing his own shoulders to shake off some of their tension.

"I prefer to simply call it confidence," he stated, matching her smile.

She stuck her hand out. "Zara Olsen."

He took her hand. It was soft, but the shake held strength. "Emmett Strong."

She tossed her head back and laughed. She had a great laugh. "Your last name is *Strong?*"

He knew his grin was goofy, but he didn't care. He liked how he felt around this woman. He liked her. "Yep. Told ya, I'd whoop you at an arm-wrestle. My name doesn't lie."

"Well, if that's what we're doing here, my last name isn't Olsen, it's *Brilliant*. Zara Brilliant." She thrust her hand forward once again. "Pleased to make your acquaintance."

Oh, yeah, he definitely liked her. Pretty and witty—a winning combo if ever there was one.

Twenty years ago, when he was an undergrad on the prowl in a hopping night club, he would have been a drunk idiot and thrown out a line like *"Your last name should be Gorgeous."* But he was too smart for that shit now. He shook his head at the memory of how much of a pussy-obsessed beast he'd been. He'd do his best to keep JoJo away from guys like him. His ego back then could have eclipsed the sun.

He fought the urge to shudder at the embarrassing memories.

He wasn't that guy now.

He'd grown up. He'd matured. He'd become a father to a

beautiful little girl who he wanted to wrap in bubble wrap and shield from any and all heartache.

Zara lifted a dark eyebrow at him. "You okay there, *Mr. Strongman?*" Her very full lips wiggled at one corner as she tried not to smile.

Emmett's chest shook, and he grinned back at her. "Yep, just telling the twenty-year-old in me to *not* say the line I would have said two decades ago." Oh, why did he reveal that? Now she'd want to know what he was thinking.

Curiosity stole across her features, and she opened her mouth, but they were saved by the barista. "Extra-large black coffee, double espresso shot and an everything bagel with cream cheese, lox and cucumber," the male barista said, interrupting their banter.

Oh, thank God.

Emmett inclined his head forward to offer Zara the coffee and bagel first and was about to say something like "After you" when the barista plunked the duplicates down and said, "Times two."

They each reached for their coffees and breakfasts. Emmett's knuckles brushed hers just as they wrapped their fingers around their enormous to-go coffee cups, and a surge of something he could only define as electric attraction sprinted from his hand straight down between his legs.

"Enjoy your breakfast, Mr. *Strong*," Zara said, once again tossing her head back and laughing as she made to leave. She shot him a smile over her shoulder and shook her head, chuckling as she heaved the door open and headed down the sidewalk.

Why hadn't he asked her to sit and have breakfast with him? Why hadn't he asked for her number? Why had he just stood there like an idiot and smiled like an idiot and flirted like an idiot, allowing the most beautiful and interesting woman he'd met in a long while walk right out the door?

Because you're scared. You thought Tiff was the love of your life, your soul mate, and she fucking ripped your heart out and stomped on it. You don't want that to happen again.

Fuck you. I'm not scared.

Well, you're talking to yourself ... so you're at the very least a little crazy.

Grumbling, he brought his coffee cup to his lips and took a sip, allowing the caffeine to flood his veins and wake him up. He made his way through the throng of people to the front door. The wind was strong, but thankfully it was only a hop, skip and a five-minute walk to the hospital. Hopefully, he wouldn't get blown away on his way there. Hopefully, he'd run into Zara again.

And what are you going to do if you do see her? Challenge her to an arm-wrestle?

Maybe. Was that such a bad idea? At least he'd get to touch her again.

Emmett groaned. Now he was behaving like a lovesick preteen. He wasn't sure if this was better or worse than the horny twenty-year-old.

He zipped his winter coat all the way up to his neck, put his head down and took off in the direction of work. Maybe sewing people up and treating broken limbs for the next nine hours would put him in a better mood, keep him from thinking about his lonely life and his ex-wife off with Huntley the Moron.

It was New Year's Eve, and the ER was going to be crazy.

It was New Year's Eve, and Emmett had no one.

It was New Year's Eve—next year had to be better.

Tomorrow had to be better.

ZARA RAN through the automatic doors of the hospital, her

hand wrapped in a paper towel pressed tightly to her chest. It had started to sleet, and her hair stuck to the sides of her face and neck. She hadn't had time—or been able—to throw her coat on, so she shivered as she approached the front desk. "I've cut my hand really badly, and I need some help, please," she said to the tired-looking woman in her late fifties.

The woman's fingers continued to *tippity-tap* on the computer. She also didn't bother to look up from her computer screen. "Go sit down, and someone will be with you shortly."

Zara's eyes went wide. The hospital waiting room was packed to the rafters. People sneezed and sniffled, coughed and wheezed in every corner. She fought the urge to lift the collar of her shirt over her nose and mouth out of fear of catching something.

But that was the least of her concerns at the moment. Her concern was her hand and the fact it hadn't stopped bleeding. She knew she had to hold it above her heart, and she was doing the best she could, but trying to finish up bouquet orders before the flower shop closed for the night—for the year—was a bit tough with one hand.

"I really need to see a doctor," she pleaded, a trickle of blood escaping the paper towel and meandering its way down her wrist.

The woman behind the desk finally lifted her sullen gray eyes away from the computer screen and fixed them on Zara. "You and everybody else behind you. Now either go to the ER down the corridor or take a seat. There are only so many doctors in the clinic today and they see people in order of arrival, *not* based on priority." She held Zara's gaze for a half second longer, her mouth dipped into a frown, and then she pretended that Zara was no longer there and went back to her computer.

Zara's eyes flicked up to the sign above the desk. *Free Clinic.*

She needed the emergency room. This was an emergency, after all. God, why did they design hospitals like freaking labyrinths? How was anybody supposed to get where they needed to go before they bled out? Or worse, got so lost they died of old age simply trying to find the giftshop.

With both arms up in the air now, the injured one and the other one holding the paper towel in place, she walked at a brisk pace down the hall toward the big yellow and red sign that said *Emergency Room.*

She was nearly there when a door opened in front of her, hitting her in the face—and the hand.

She fell backward onto her butt, the paper towel flying behind her and blood droplets coating the wall.

"Whoa!" came a gentle voice. "You okay?"

Zara blinked and blinked before she levered herself up onto her elbows and lifted her head to find none other than Mr. Strong from the coffee shop staring down at her.

Recognition immediately dawned on him. He smiled, that is until his eyes took in her bloody and bleeding hand and the fresh spray of blood on the walls. His smile faded.

A look of concern flooded his face. "You're hurt," he said, worry in his tone. He helped her up with a gentle hand under her arm and grabbed the paper towel, quickly placing it back over her sliced hand to stanch the blood flow.

With one hand at the small of her back and another holding her injured hand, he led her down the hall from where she'd come, but before they got back to the desk where Nurse Crankypants sat, he took a hard right into an empty exam room.

"Hop up on the table there and let's take a look," he said, closing the door, then wandering over to the small corner counter sink and washing his hands. "What happened?

"I cut my hand on a vase," she said, watching him move around the small exam room. He dried his hands and pulled on a pair of blue latex gloves before he made his way back over to her and picked up her hand. She winced as he peeled away the paper towel and turned her hand around in his.

He sucked in a breath through clenched teeth. "You certainly did cut your hand. Yikes!"

She rolled her eyes. "I'm such an idiot."

"I highly doubt that," he said, pulling a drawer open next to him and beginning to rummage around. "Even geniuses get hurt from time to time. I highly doubt Einstein never skinned his knee or bumped his funny bone."

A smile turned up at the corner of her mouth. "Maybe not. But I should know better. I was trying to do too many things at once."

He was preparing a syringe. He handed her a piece of fresh gauze. "Hold this on the cut, please."

She did as she was told, mesmerized by the way he moved so confidently, his hands sure and capable.

Then it hit her. Not only was his last name *Strong,* he was a freaking doctor to boot.

Zara snorted.

He lifted his head. "Something funny?"

She snorted again. "I just realized you're *Dr. Strong.*"

"The one and only ... in this hospital anyway."

"Do you moonlight as an astronaut? Are you *Astronaut Dr. Strong*? Because I honestly don't know what else you could do or be to make yourself any more ... "

He lifted one dark eyebrow, which seemed to also pull at the same corner of his mouth. "Any more ... "

She lifted then flopped her free hand down to the exam table. "I dunno ... appealing? Handsome? A catch?"

Was she coming on too strong?

Too freaking bad.

Zara had never been shy a day in her life, nor was she the type to beat around the bush and not say what she was thinking.

She found the man attractive. There was no reason why she couldn't say that. Right?

The other corner of his mouth lifted as well. "I like your candor ... but I can attest that not every woman thinks I'm appealing or a catch."

Then those women are crazy.

She kept that thought to herself. There was speaking your mind and then there was coming on too strong. She was known for doing both.

"I don't moonlight as an astronaut," he said, pushing the bottom of the syringe up just a touch and making a small amount of liquid squirt out. He brought it over to her and removed the gauze. "This might hurt a little. But I'm going to numb the area before I apply the sutures."

Zara swallowed and nodded. "Okay. I've been through childbirth. A little sting is nothing compared to that."

His chuckle was deep and throaty. "That's the spirit." He gripped her hand. "Hold still."

She did as she was told.

"I do, however, moonlight as a cop," he joked, gently sliding the tip of the syringe into her hand. "Have to pay those med school student loans somehow." He pulled the syringe free and then placed the gauze back over the cut that was still bleeding.

"So you're *Officer Dr. Strong?*" she asked.

He nodded. "Well, actually *Captain Dr. Strong.* But you can just call me *Officer.* Captain just seems so formal."

She rolled her eyes at his teasing tone and smirk.

"Ah, what the heck. You can call me Emmett." He removed the gauze and pressed around the area. "How does that feel? Numb yet?"

She didn't feel a damn thing. "Yup."

He smiled. "Good." He plunked his butt down on a round rolling stool and opened up a drawer beneath the exam table, pulling out a suture kit. "So you have kids?"

Zara held her hand still on her lap, watching the top of his head as he prepared the suture like he'd done it a million times before—which he probably had.

He lifted his head. "Kids?"

Right.

"I have a son," she said, feeling the heat in her cheeks travel down her neck and up into her hairline. "He's seven." She was too transfixed by the handsome man in front of her to think straight.

She'd also lost a lot of blood.

Yeah, blood loss. That's why she was acting like an idiot. It had nothing to do with hot Dr. Strong and his luscious head of short, dark, curly hair or his dark amber eyes. And those eyelashes—she paid good money every three weeks to get eyelashes like that.

And that smell. Oh so manly, oh so fresh. How did he stay smelling that yummy in a hospital?

"I have a daughter," he said, taking her hand and resting it next to her on the crinkly paper of the exam table. "She's almost six."

"What's her name?" Zara asked. They needed to keep talking, otherwise she was going to lean over and smell his hair or at the very least run her free hand through it. It looked really thick. She loved a man with a good, thick head of hair.

"Josephine," he said, lifting the gauze away from her hand. "But we call her Josie or JoJo."

We.

So he was married.

"What's your son's name?" He pushed the tip of the suture

needle into her skin and began to close up the gnarly slice in her hand between her thumb and index finger. Thank freaking God it was her right hand—she was left-handed.

"Nolan," she replied. "He used to call himself NoNo when he was learning to talk. It kind of stuck as a nickname for a while."

Emmett lifted his head. "I like that. JoJo and NoNo." He jerked his chin toward her other hand, which rested on the top of her thigh. "You left-handed or right-handed?"

"Left-handed, thankfully. Otherwise I'd be in *big* trouble."

"Ah, a southpaw. JoJo is a southpaw too."

"We're pretty awesome people, us lefties."

"Can't argue with that."

He had such a calming presence to him, a gentle touch and a steady hand. She wondered how she'd never run into him before if he worked at the hospital and she worked just down the block at her flower shop.

"Any big plans for tonight?" he asked, continuing to stitch her up.

"I've been invited to a friend's party. Nothing crazy—at least, I hope. Just a few people sitting around eating and drinking. Kid-friendly too, which is nice, because Nolan's dad has to work."

"What does your husband do for work?" He pulled the last stitch through, tied it like an expert and used the stainless-steel scissors to trim the end.

"Nolan's father isn't my husband. He's my best friend, and he's gay."

Why was she telling him this?

Because you want him to know you're single.

He put away the suture kit, closed the drawer, then pulled off his gloves. He also hadn't said anything. Was he waiting for her to continue explaining?

"We've been best friends since grade school. We dated—

or at least tried to. Lost our virginity together, and that's kind of how he realized he was gay—a bit of a blow to my ego, but I got over it."

Emmett's chuckle was quiet, but his smile was warm and sexy as hell. The heat in his gaze made flames flicker and dance in her belly. The small hairs on her arms stood up, sending a prickle along her skin.

She gulped before she continued, "We made a pact that if by the time we were thirty-six and neither of us were married or had kids, we'd have one together. Raise the baby together."

He sat back down on the rolling chair and faced her, his eyes curious, his mouth set into a kind, small smile.

"I got married at twenty-seven but was divorced by thirty-four. We never had kids. Turns out my ex didn't want them. So when I turned thirty-six, I decided I didn't want to wait any longer to be a mom. Michael and I had Nolan a year later. We lived together, raised him together. Until he met Shane and they got married. Then they moved a few blocks away, and now we share custody of our son and the three of us are raising Nolan."

"It's hard at first, isn't it?" he asked. "The whole shared custody thing. Not seeing your kid every day, having to rely on phone calls and video chat."

Was he divorced too?

"My ex-wife and I separated over a year ago, and it was really hard at first not seeing JoJo every day. Really, really hard. But then it got easier, and now I make the most of my time with her, but I also enjoy the breaks where I have time to myself and I don't have to be on constant dad duty."

Zara grinned.

He got it.

This was exactly how she felt as well. She loved her kid-free moments, when she could grab a drink with a girlfriend in the evening after work or sleep in and not have to get up and make anybody breakfast. She'd never trade Nolan for anything in the world, but it was nice having some time to herself as well.

Sometimes you needed to miss your kid.

Nobody should be around another person twenty-four seven. Even your own children. Personal space and alone time were just as important as getting enough exercise and drinking six to eight glasses of water a day.

Mental health was no joke.

We all needed to engage in more self-care.

"How often do you get your daughter?" she asked, wanting to know more about the hot doctor, wanting to keep talking to him.

"Three nights one week, four nights the next. My ex-wife is a dermatologist at a private clinic, so her hours are pretty set in stone. Mine are a bit more all over the map here, but I try to keep it as consistent as possible." His eyes twinkled. "Being an attending helps." He reached for her hand. "Let's take a look at this."

He'd removed his gloves, so now it was skin against skin. His hands were big and warm and his fingers long and skilful. Zara swallowed hard and shifted where she sat at the thought of those fingers working magic into the balls of her toes, her tired, achy, shoulders, the knots in her neck ... and most definitely further south as well. His touch was not only kind, but it was strong and confident, capable and with a warmth that reminded her of a hearth fire in a stone castle. Inviting and protective. Powerful and consuming.

He brushed his thumb lightly over his stitches. "They don't seem too raised. Shouldn't bother you. Might get a little itchy." He opened up the drawer beneath the table again and drew out a roll of gauze. "I'll wrap it up in case it starts to bleed at all again. Keep it clean. You'll need to go to see your primary physician to get the stitches removed in a couple of weeks."

He held her wrist with one hand and began to wrap the gauze with the other. His eyes flicked up to hers. "What do you do for work that caused you to be carrying a big vase?"

"I'm a—"

A buzzing in his pocket made her pause.

Holding the gauze against her hand with one hand, he reached into his pocket with the other and pulled out his phone. "Shit," he muttered. "I gotta go. I'm sorry."

She waved her left hand. "No, no. Go save lives. Go reattach limbs, put guts back where they belong. It's your job. Thank *you* for stitching me up. I really appreciate it."

Smiling, though clearly distracted by whatever he'd read on his phone, he grabbed a roll of medical tape to secure the gauze, then stood up. "Take care, Zara," he said, his hand on the doorknob. "And try not to carry any more vases for a while." Then with a smile that melted her insides to goo, and made heat pool in her core, he opened the door and was gone, leaving Zara sitting there with a wrapped-up hand and a goofy smile on her face, wondering how and when she was going to see him again.

2

EMMETT OPENED his locker in the attendings' locker room and hung up his name badge and stethoscope. The door behind him opened and in sauntered—yes, sauntered, because the man had quite the swagger—Riley McMillan.

Riley grinned his cocky smile and patted Emmett on the back. "You still coming tonight, buddy? Daisy's been working her little buns off getting the house ready for tonight. Hired caterers, waitstaff, a bartender, the works. You know how my wife likes to throw a party."

"Only reason I'm coming," Emmett said, running his hand through his hair and checking his face in the mirror on the inside of his locker door. He looked tired, but nothing a shower couldn't fix. "Your wife always throws the best parties —and by best, I mean she hires the best caterers in town and you have an open bar."

Riley opened up his locker and slouched out of his white doctor's coat. "Tonight's party is going to be great." His sly grin made the hair on the back of Emmett's neck stand up. Daisy always had a trick or two up her sleeve—the woman was a professional matchmaker, after all. Was this one of *those* parties?

Why hadn't he thought of that possibility sooner?

"What's your woman got up her sleeve this time?" Emmett asked, pushing his arms into the sleeves of his winter coat and zipping it up. "I'm not interested in being set up if this is her angle tonight. JoJo is going to be there, and you all know how I feel about introducing my kid to someone I'm dating too soon. Just 'cause my ex did it doesn't mean I'm going to put my kid through that."

Riley rolled his eyes. "Dating and simply meeting someone to see if there is a spark are two very different things. Besides, the kids are going to be downstairs in the playroom with a babysitter."

Emmett squeezed his molars together in an attempt to tamp down the bubbling anger that now ran hot through his veins. "I don't fucking like being set up. I've told your wife that."

Riley sat down on the bench and untied his running shoes. "It's not a *setup*." He lifted his head and squinted his dark brown eyes. His baby face, with rosy cheeks, lost the cocky smile and suddenly turned serious. "Do you need to head to The Rage Room before tonight? Got a chip on that shoulder of yours again there, buddy?"

The Rage Room was a new business in town that specialized in smashing the shit out of anything and everything from furniture to dishes, appliances to vases. For fifty bucks you could rent a room for thirty minutes and demolish everything inside with your weapon of choice. Emmett liked the aluminum baseball bat, though he also found the crowbar oddly satisfying.

Emmett slung his computer bag over his shoulder and grunted. "No. Besides, I think Luna closed The Rage Room tonight for a private party."

"On a first-name basis with the proprietor there, are you?" Riley asked, pulling his shiny black dress shoes out from beneath the bench and slipping his feet into them. The cocky grin was back on his stupid face. "What about asking her out?"

"I don't think she bats for our team," Emmett said dryly. "Besides, even if she did, I'm not interested in dating right now. JoJo and work are enough for me."

Then why can't you get Zara and her expressive blue eyes out of your head? Who are you kidding? It isn't her eyes, although they are beautiful. You're thinking about the way her soaking wet sweater clung to her sexy frame, showing off everything she had to offer—and more.

Riley rolled his eyes. "Keep telling yourself that, bud." He stood up and reached into his locker for his winter coat, sliding his arms into the sleeves. "Just leave the bad attitude at home tonight, all right? My wife has gone to a shit-ton of trouble to plan a nice party, and I won't have your crappy-ass mood ruining it for her. Best friend or not, I will cart your ass out of my house if I find you getting snarky with the other guests."

Emmett lifted one eyebrow at his friend. Riley was only about an inch and a half taller than Emmett, but Emmett was bigger. Zak, one of the fellow Single Dads of Seattle, owned Club Z Fitness, and all the single dads got discounted memberships—not that Riley was a single dad, but he went to Club Z too. Emmett had started going to the gym on the regular when JoJo was in school and he wasn't working. Zak had helped him bulk up and start lifting a pretty impressive weight—well, at least Emmett was impressed with himself. Zak could bench-press a fucking Chevy Sprint.

Emmett stood toe to toe with his best friend. Riley's brows narrowed, his mouth in a thin line.

Emmett twisted his lips and cocked a brow.

"I'll stand here as long as I have to until you promise not to ruin my wife's party," Riley said blandly, a lock of his blond hair falling over his forehead. His nickname among their group of doctor friends was *pretty boy* for good reason.

Emmett nodded once. "I promise."

"Go get her some flowers," Riley said, breaking their intense eye contact and slinging his computer bag over his shoulder. "Chicks like flowers."

Emmett snorted, and the two men headed toward the door. "Your wife okay with you calling her a *chick?*"

Riley was all grins again. "My wife's got me by the balls, man. If she wanted me to call her *queen,* I would. I'm the luckiest son of a bitch in the world to be married to Daisy."

Emmett didn't disagree. Riley's wife was one of the sweetest human beings on Earth.

"No argument here, man," Emmett said, falling in line with Riley as they made their way through the hospital. "And I promise not to ruin Daisy's party with my bad attitude. I'll go into tonight with an open mind and big smile." He flashed the cheesiest smile he could muster at his friend.

How many times did he need to say it out loud for it to become true?

A million?

A trillion?

Riley snorted. "Don't forget the flowers. There's a flower shop on the corner Daisy likes."

"Do I get her daisies?"

The automatic doors opened, and they both walked through, the cold winter air hitting them like a bitch-slap in the face. Snow littered the ground from a couple of freak blizzards last week, and the scent of another snowfall lingered in the air.

Zara had been soaked to the skin when she'd come in,

and evidence of a slushy rain showed on all the car wind-shields in the parking lot. Thankfully, it wasn't raining now.

"She likes ranunculus and peonies," Riley said as they made their way into the parking lot, breaking Emmett out of his train of thought—the Zara train.

Emmett screwed up his face and hit the fob to unlock his SUV. "What the fuck are those?"

Riley had parked right next to Emmett and hit the fob for his BMW SUV. "Fuck if I know. I just know that's what I order and by the bucketload when I've fucked up."

"Which is a lot?" Emmett asked, chuckling to himself.

"Not lately, thank God," Riley replied.

Emmett tossed his computer bag into the back seat of his SUV. "All right then. I guess I'm off to go buy a nice lady some flowers." He relocked his vehicle, figuring he'd just walk to the flower shop rather than risk not finding any street parking.

Riley swung his big frame in behind his steering wheel, but not before calling out, "It's my party too, you know. And I much prefer scotch to flowers."

Emmett glanced behind him and flashed his friend the middle finger.

Riley was all smiles and laughs. "Macallan 18, please, *Dr. Strong.* I know you can afford it. I know how much money you make."

"Yeah, but I also have to pay alimony and child support," Emmett shot back.

"I still know you can afford to get your good buddy his favorite bottle," Riley called out into wind.

Emmett didn't bother to turn around as he headed out of the parking lot, but he did lift his other hand in the air behind him and flipped the bird with both fingers this time.

"Make it Macallan 25, jackass."

Thankfully, the flower shop Riley was referring to was

only a block and a half up the street from the hospital. Emmett knew it well, though he had never been inside. It was a Seattle staple—been on that corner with that same dark green awning and gold lettering for as long as he could remember. It even said "Flowers on 5th Est. 1935," so it'd been there a long while.

He put his head down and pulled the collar of his coat tighter around his neck to avoid getting any more strong, freezing gusts down his shirt. A few rogue flurries hit his face, and he glanced up at the sky. It was already dark out, and there wasn't a star to be seen.

New Year's Eve with a snowstorm. He could only imagine that the hospital was going to be a zoo later that night.

The green awning came into view, and he picked up the pace. He still needed to go grab JoJo from Tiff's and then head home and jump into the shower. He hoped his ex had enough sense to feed JoJo before Emmett picked her up. That wasn't always the case though, and then JoJo would complain that she was hungry and Emmett would scramble to feed her when they got home.

He always sent JoJo to Tiff with a full belly and clean clothes in her bag.

Courtesy must have gone out the window the moment the ink was dry on the divorce papers. He certainly knew the love was gone.

He heaved open the door of the florist's shop, causing the bell to chime, and stepped inside, immediately feeling better. He inhaled, allowing the scent of all the fragrant flowers to calm his nerves. He always got tense when he thought about his ex.

"Be right with you," called a friendly female voice from the back room.

"No rush," he replied. Even though he kind of was in a rush. He began to wander around the enormous space, taking in all the various premade bouquets sitting in black buckets filled with water. He hadn't a clue what each bud or bloom was, but they were certainly pretty.

He glanced in the direction of the back room and cash register. A large stuffed bear in a floral printed dress sat collecting dust up on a shelf—it immediately reminded him of his own stuffed bear, Dr. Arnold Strong, sitting on his bookshelf at home. He wondered if the bear behind the counter had as much meaning to whoever put it there.

Smiling at the bear for another half second, he turned back around, shoved his hands in his pockets and began to wander again. A peony or ranunculus could have smacked him upside the head and he'd never know it.

He could identify every muscle, bone, organ, tendon and ligament in the human body, but heaven help him if he was forced to discern between a petunia and a begonia. They might as well all be roses as far as he was concerned.

"Ah, sorry about that. What can I do for you?" came the same voice from the back, only this time, it was directly behind him.

"I'm looking for ranunculus and peonies, please." Emmett spun around. His eyes went wide, and the smile that stretched across his mouth hurt his face. "It's you!"

Her smile was equally big—breathtaking, actually—and her blue eyes twinkled. "It's me."

"I didn't know you were a florist." He nodded. "That explains the vase."

Zara continued to grin. "It does. I was about to tell you what I did when you were paged to the ER to go and save a life."

"I saved like ten actually," he said, loving the way her eyes crinkled at the corner when she was being cheeky. The page had actually been about a gunshot wound in the abdomen, and the guy survived.

He hoped she knew he was just kidding.

"Oh, well, then, it's a good thing you ran away from me when you did."

"I'd never intentionally run away from you."

Whoa! Where did that come from?

"Unless it was to save lives, though, right?"

His smile just kept getting bigger. "Right."

Was this flirting?

He hadn't flirted in so long, he couldn't remember what it felt like.

He'd been a master flirter back in the day—or at least he liked to think he had been. Was flirting the same now?

Was he doing it right?

Was she flirting with him too?

"So, ranunculus and peonies, huh?" she asked. "Those are not in season, so they run a pretty penny. Must be a very special person you're giving these to."

She showed him her back and headed toward a small walk-in cooler. He followed her.

"My friend's wife. She's throwing a New Year's Eve party tonight, and he told me to bring her flowers. He's worried my grumpy ass will ruin the party, so he wants me to show up with a peace offering."

"Why are you grumpy?" She grabbed a black bucket, then pointed at another one on a small wire rack. "Grab those peonies there, please."

It was a cramped space with the two of them in there as well as all the buckets and flowers. They had to do a little shuffle dance for him to get around her. The side of her hips brushed his, then her elbow on his waist. He wasn't sure if it was the flowers or her, but something smelled incredible.

He did as he was told and picked up the bucket of peonies, following her out of the cool room and back toward the desk.

"Just plop them right there, please."

He did as instructed, then took a step back to watch the master at work.

"So, hmmm, why are you grumpy? I can do two things at once, you know. Make a bouquet and talk." She carefully began to pull individual blooms out of the bucket and lay them out on a shiny piece of gold paper.

"No reason," he started. "His wife is a matchmaker, and I have the sneaking suspicion she's hosting a matchmaking party. I've told the woman several times to *not* try to set me up."

Zara nodded. "Ah, I getcha now. But you're still going to go?"

Emmett shoved his hands into his pants pockets. "Yeah. He's my best friend, and she's one of the nicest people in the world. Besides, the food spread they put out is some of the best grub I will eat all damn year. And it'll have an open bar." He shrugged. "Kind of a no-brainer."

She shrugged as well but didn't look up from what she was doing. "Obviously. You'll just have to resist the advances of all the eligible bachelorettes who are eager to sink their painted nails into a handsome doctor like you."

Emmett's bottom lip dropped open.

Zara still hadn't lifted her head. "I don't know a woman alive who wouldn't want to land a doctor."

Emmett snorted. "I can probably name a few."

Finally, she drew her gaze from the bouquet and up to his face. Her cornflower-blue eyes had grown serious. "Perhaps, but doctor or not, I can tell you're a catch. You better watch yourself tonight." Then the corner of her mouth lifted up into a lopsided smile. "Or you might just fall in love and get your happily ever after."

Heat raced through his veins as he stood there and blinked.

But instead of getting all flustered, Zara simply tossed her head back and laughed. "Or not," she said lightly. "Looks to me like you'd run in the opposite direction from love. Been burned that badly, huh?"

She turned around and grabbed a few pieces of green foliage from a table behind her, then laid them down with the rest of the blossoms.

"Can't say I blame you if that's the case," she went on. "I thought I'd found the one, married him. Gave him some of the best years of my life—my most fertile years—then he decided kids weren't his jam, and that was that." She snorted. "Would you believe me if I told you he found some little hottie at Chili's and knocked her up on their third date, not six months after our divorce was final?" Fire burned in her eyes. A pain. An anger.

She gathered up the bouquet and then began to fold the paper over.

"I'm sorry," Emmett said quietly, his hand landing on hers before he could stop himself.

She looked up from what she was doing, pain swirling behind the glint of frustration in her eyes. He could feel her waves of ire. They were just radiating off her.

"That wasn't fair to you at all. Your ex was an idiot."

"*Is* an idiot," she corrected. "He's not dead—as much as I sometimes wish he was. Bastard has two kids with *Tobi*—with an *I*—because she'll tell you. 'I'm *Tobi—with an I*,'" Zara said in a baby-doll voice at the same time she tilted her head to the side and cocked her hip. "'I'm Tobi, with and *I* and I have the IQ of a lemon wedge.'"

Laughter burst through Emmett's nose. "A lemon wedge?"

She rolled her eyes. "You have a love for lemons or something? A rock then? She has the IQ of a rock."

He snorted.

She rolled those brilliant blue eyes again, her sour

expression turning sweet the longer she held his gaze. A chuckle bubbled up from her chest and buzzed past her lips. Emmett grinned wider too, and squeezed his hand, which just so happened to still be on top of hers. He'd forgotten about that.

Instantly, her gaze flew down to where they touched.

Swallowing, he smiled a closed-mouth smile and pulled his hand free. "Sorry."

She shook her head. "It's okay. I was the one who loaded all that garbage onto you—a paying customer. I should be apologizing." She grabbed a long strand of what looked like hay or something and proceeded to wrap it around the paper.

"I think we're beyond customer and proprietor, wouldn't you say?" he asked. "I mean, we're also doctor and patient and breakfast twins."

"Breakfast twins," she repeated, picking up the bouquet and presenting it to him. "I like that."

He reached for the bouquet, admiring her skill—because it was a skill. He'd never be able to take a bunch of flowers and arrange them into something so beautiful.

"Cards and envelopes are on the side of the counter there," she said, pointing to a small stand. "They're complimentary."

He nodded and grabbed one that said "Thank you."

"I hope your party goes well tonight," she said, stepping behind the cash register. "I hope you find love if you're looking for it or bypass it if you're not."

He made a noise in his throat that ended up coming off far more dismissive than he would have liked.

Emmett wasn't anti-love like his friend Liam. He just wasn't sure a soul mate existed for him anymore. He just wasn't sure love was in the cards for *him* anymore.

Tiff had ripped out his heart, and he wasn't entirely on

board with the possibility of someone doing that to him—or his daughter—again.

It also didn't help that he was a forty-year-old man and had zero interest in dating again. He was so over that shit. If he could, he'd just jump right into the movie and nacho nights at his place, curled up on his couch with a bottle of wine.

Expensive dinners in uncomfortable clothes and putting on airs was so overrated, so unrealistic and in a lot of ways boring.

Maybe Daisy is trying to save you from doing that by setting you up with your soul mate?

He pushed that thought clear out of his head, hearing it whistle as it plummeted toward the ground, only to land with a harsh but satisfying *splat.*

Could he invite Zara to the New Year's Eve party?

No. She had her own party to attend that night. She'd probably find a great guy to kiss at midnight too. Of course she would. The woman was a real looker—and smart and funny to boot.

He watched as she punched in a few keys on the keyboard. "That'll be sixty-seven fifty," she said, adding a bit of a wince to her smile.

Emmett looked up from where he'd been scribbling a note to Daisy and overthinking his entire life.

"I told you they were expensive," she said, her mouth bunched up in a purse of regret—even a face like that was beautiful on her.

His eyes bugged out as he fished into his back pocket and grabbed his wallet. "You weren't kidding." He held up his credit card. "Is that the *doctor* discount?" He nodded at her bandaged hand. "After all, I *did* save your hand. Some might say I saved your life. Certainly saved your livelihood."

Her lips twitched as she took his card. "As a matter of fact, it is. Unlike normal customers, your bouquet not only comes with a smile and a big ol' *thank you*, but I'm also throwing in some of my highly regarded sage advice—and that shit is priceless."

He swiped his card. "Oh, this I have to hear."

Zara cleared her throat at the same time she handed him her receipt. "Don't shy away from love simply because your heart has been broken. The heart mends. The heart is resilient. You are worthy of love. You are worthy of being someone's everything again. Don't waste the best years of your life angry at what was, and instead spend those years searching and hoping for what could be."

His stomach did a serious somersault—the second that day in the presence of this intriguing woman.

Zara's eyes glimmered, and she lifted one shoulder casually. "There, that's my advice. Take it or leave it, but know that I only dish it out to my VIP customers."

Emmett's head swam with something smart and articulate to say back, but for once in his forty years, he was speechless. His mouth opened, but nothing came out.

Zara's eyes flickered like two blue stars at him as a big smile spread across her face. "Have I rendered the handsome doctor speechless?" she teased.

In more ways than one.

Damn, she was something.

He hadn't met a woman like her in a long time—perhaps ever.

She said what was on her mind and wasn't ashamed to compliment him or express her interest. It was refreshing to not have to guess at her intentions or how she truly felt. She was mature and confident, and he really liked that.

He really liked her.

He needed to see this woman again. Only this time, he needed it to be planned. He needed it to be where they had more than just a couple of minutes of witty banter and meaningful eye contact. He wanted hours with her. He wanted a date.

This was the first woman he'd met since his divorce who made him want to open his heart up to the possibility of a relationship again. And as much as that excited him, it also terrified him.

He cleared his throat and opened his mouth, ready to ask her out, when the door chimed behind him and the *slap, slap* of someone—most likely a child—and their wet boots stomping on the tile floor interrupted his plans.

"Mom." The little boy with dark hair and the same eyes as his mother wasted no time ducking around behind the counter and wrapping his arms around Zara's waist. "Dad and Shane took me to see the new Dwayne Johnson movie."

Zara lifted her head, recognition flashing in her eyes. "Was that for him or you?"

"It was for everyone." A tall, lean, impeccably dressed man came to stand next to Emmett. He leaned over and peered into the bouquet. "Oh, peonies and ranunculus." His dark green eyes raked Emmett quickly but thoroughly from head to toe. "Someone's been a bad boy and needs to apologize?"

Zara snorted. "Leave him be, Michael." Her eyes softened as she fixed her gaze on Emmett. His pulse still raced from her earlier comment about not shying away from love and holding on to hope for the future. "Ignore him. He's just teasing."

Emmett nodded. "I've got to run."

But I wish I could stay.

She smiled, wrapping her arm around her son's shoulders. "Okay. It was nice to see you again. I hope your friend enjoys the flowers."

Unease and something else entirely foreign and weird

swirled around in his head. He nodded again. "Yeah, thanks. I'm sure she will." He headed toward the door, the sound of Zara, Michael and her son talking spurring him to increase his stride and make a quick exit.

"Oh and hey!" she called back.

He stopped with his hand on the door handle and turned to face her.

"Happy New Year, *Officer Astronaut Dr. Strong*." Her smile could light up an entire city.

"*Officer Astronaut Dr. Strong*?" Michael asked. "Is there such a thing?"

Emmett simply waved and muttered a halfhearted "You too" before retreating into the dark, freezing evening—the final night of the year—to the echo of Zara's breathy and feminine laughter. His brain felt fuzzy and his body hot.

His heart, though—his heart was crystal-clear and steady. His heart knew beyond a shadow of a doubt that he needed to see Zara Olsen again.

3

EMMETT GLANCED down at his daughter in her cute little red peacoat, black sparkling shoes and white and black plaid dress as they precariously placed one foot in front of the other and made their way up Daisy and Riley's steep and icy driveway. A Seattle mansion waited for them at the top.

Josie picked out her own outfit and, as she put it, this outfit was *party perfect*. Her stuffed giraffe Zelda was clutched tight between her elbow and chest, her comfort toy and one she'd had since birth. Zelda had certainly seen better days and at the moment could probably use a wash, but if JoJo could help it, she never went anywhere without her companion.

Emmett had been the same way when he was a boy. Only his comfort item had been a stuffed bear named Arnold, and Arnold wore a T-shirt made out of Emmett's grandfather's old doctor coat, complete with the stitched *Dr. Strong* on the left side. His grandfather died three days before Emmett was born, and Emmett was also named after him.

Officially, he was Emmett Harold Strong II. Named for both of his grandfathers—Emmett Strong and Harold Abernathy—who had passed before he was born, but who still carried heavy influence over his life. Both men had been doctors, just like Emmett's father had been. Healing was in his blood. It was his calling—always had been. Healing, fixing, safety, security. They were as intrinsic in his life as the nose on his face. He still had a back pocket full of Band-Aids, never went anywhere without them—and hadn't since his friend's first scraped knee when they were seven and riding their bikes down the street to the park when Raphe had bailed on the gravel.

Arnold the bear was Dr. Arnold Strong, and he stood for everything Emmett was, where he came from and where he intended to go.

That bear now sat in his home office, on a bookshelf, with a healthy coat of dust on him. But he was still in Emmett's life. He liked to think that his grandfather Emmett Senior was watching him through the eyes of Arnold, keeping Emmett safe and on track.

He thought back to the bear in Zara's flower shop. Was that Zara's bear? Did it have a story to it as well? Was it her childhood comfort toy?

"Why are you bringing Aunt Daisy flowers?" JoJo asked, her hand squeezing Emmett's tight as her foot slipped on a slick patch of black ice. "It's not her birthday."

He held her hand even tighter and hauled her up before she fell, both of their eyes going wide.

Phew.

They continued on their journey. "I'm bringing Aunt Daisy flowers because it's a nice thing to do. When you're invited over to someone's house for dinner or a party, it's rude to show up empty-handed. You either bring a gift for the host or hostess or something to contribute to the meal."

"So that bottle of *booze* is for the meal?"

He loved the way she said *booze.*

"It's for Uncle Riley. It's his favorite. After all, they're *both* our hosts."

Her nose wrinkled up along with the rest of her face. "Should I have brought them something?" Panic filled her green eyes. "I mean, I'm eating here too, right? A gift for Nick?"

Emmett chuckled. "Nick's three. I think he'll be happy if you just play with him. Besides, you're my date. My host gifts are your host gifts. I'll share."

JoJo let out a big exhale, her shoulders slumping at the same time she released Emmett's hand. "Oh, thank goodness. I was worried. I mean I could have drawn them a picture, I suppose. I can still do that if Aunt Daisy will loan me some crayons."

Staring down at his precious and thoughtful daughter, Emmett bent down to kiss her on the top of the head. "Don't worry, JoJo-bean, you just enjoy the party. My host gifts are enough for both of them." He tickled the back of her neck. "Want to push the doorbell?"

She grinned up at him and nodded. Daisy and Riley had a very melodic and sing-song doorbell that JoJo absolutely loved. She lifted up on her tiptoes and reached up to press the fancy illuminated bell.

Everything in Riley and Daisy's house was fancy.

Daisy had expensive taste.

And why not? Her matchmaking business was a huge success; the woman could afford her expensive taste, even without her husband's doctor salary.

The tune chimed throughout the house, making JoJo giggle. "Can I press it again?" she asked, extending up onto her tiptoes once more.

Emmett shook his head and was about to say "once is enough" when the big, solid oak door swung open, revealing a smiling Daisy in a very tight, very pretty gold dress.

"Happy New Year, Josie, sweetheart," Daisy said, welcoming them inside and immediately wrapping her shapely arms around Emmett's daughter.

Daisy had known JoJo from birth. In fact, she and Riley were JoJo's godparents, so there was no shyness or hiding behind his leg.

His daughter hugged Daisy back. "Happy New Year, Aunt Daisy. Where's Nick? Where's Chelsea?"

You'd never know Daisy had given birth not five months ago. The woman had dropped the baby weight with a snap of her fingers.

"Chelsea is with the babysitter downstairs. I'm sure she's in the baby carrier. It's where she prefers to be these days. And Nick is downstairs as well. Last time I checked, all the kids were quite engrossed in an episode of *PAW Patrol.*"

JoJo's nose wrinkled and her mouth contorted into a scrunched frown. "I'm too old for *PAW Patrol.* I *am* almost six, you know. I'm in kindergarten, and kindergarteners are too old for *PAW Patrol.*"

Emmett's lips flattened and squeezed together as he fought the urge to laugh, his gaze meeting Daisy's over his daughter's head.

Daisy grinned at him before dropping down to a crouch, which was a task in and of itself, given her tight dress.

"Well, you know what, Josie, there are *other* things to do downstairs besides watch the television. I've also told Nick and the babysitter that the TV can't be on the whole time. There is also coloring, cookie decorating, puppets, puzzles. I set the easel up in the laundry room, so you're welcome to paint."

Josie suddenly retreated a couple of steps backward and wrapped her arm around Emmett's leg, glancing up at him with her big, green eyes. "I don't want to go down alone, Daddy."

Emmett exhaled through his nose and ran his hand down his daughter's silky, soft blonde hair. "I'll come down with you for a bit, sweetie. Help you settle in."

Her voice dropped to a whisper. "Thanks, Dad."

"Not a problem at all," Daisy said, her tone chipper. "I'm sure you'll be having fun in no time." She stepped toward them, her arms out. "Let me take your coats, and then you two head downstairs. There are only a handful of people here so far, so you won't miss anything."

"Dad, the flowers!" JoJo piped up. She faced Daisy. "We have host gifts for you and Uncle Riley. You get flowers. Uncle Riley gets *booze*."

Daisy's smile was big and warm. She laughed as Emmett thrust the bouquet into her arms, the gift bag with the bottle of scotch for Riley still hanging from his fingers.

Daisy dipped her head to smell the flowers, her green eyes closing. "Mmmm, peonies and ranunculus, my favorites. This bouquet is gorgeous."

JoJo beamed. "It's from both of us, just so you know."

Emmett rolled his eyes and hid his smile by turning his head. This kid ...

Daisy turned around and rested the bouquet on the stairs. "Well, they're gorgeous. Thank you *so* much, Josie, for your very thoughtful host gift."

JoJo's smile was bigger than life.

Daisy offered to take their coats, starting with Emmett.

"Thanks," Emmett murmured as he unbuttoned his wool coat and slipped his arms out of it, letting Daisy take it from him and hang it up in the closet off the foyer. She did the same for JoJo.

"No worries," Daisy said with a chuckle. "I'm sure Josie will be comfortable in just a few minutes, telling you to *vamoose* in no time."

"Let's hope so," he muttered back as he took his daughter's cool, delicate hand. He glanced down at her. "Shall we?"

JoJo's eyes held a nervous apprehension that pulled at every string in his heart. If his daughter wasn't having fun, they would be out of there. He wasn't going to ruin her new year simply to appease his matchmaking friends.

He handed off the gift bag to Daisy as well before he let JoJo lead him down the stairs to the basement, where the sound of laughing children drew them like the pied piper.

TWENTY MINUTES LATER, Emmett climbed the stairs to the top floor of Riley and Daisy's house. As expected, JoJo had settled right in. She found a couple of little girls close to her age, and the three of them were all sitting at a table making beaded necklaces.

JoJo loved bling, so she'd probably spend the entire night there and then come home with enough necklaces for her entire kindergarten class.

Riley spied Emmett and met him at the top of the stairs, slapping him on the back. "I'm glad to see you didn't get entranced by *PAW Patrol* and decide to ring in the new year with the sticky-handed monkeys downstairs."

Emmett smirked. "I've seen that episode probably ten dozen times. *I* could reenact it verbatim. Thank God JoJo is done with that phase."

Riley chuckled. "It only means a new one is on the way."

Emmett exhaled. "Don't I know it. Where's the booze?"

Riley's grin was close-mouthed but wide. "Right this way, sir. Though I tucked that *very* generous and *thoughtful* host gift JoJo brought me in my bedroom."

Emmett snorted and followed his friend through the festive but tastefully decorated house toward the dining room.

"Don't want the bartender mistaking that for something I'm willing to share with the likes of *these* people." Riley lifted his dark blond eyebrow toward the rather full living room. "I hardly know half these people—besides those from the hospital. The rest are all people Daisy knows who are single and she wants to help find love. I'm not giving them my Macallan 18 for free."

"You better not. You know how much that shit costs. You better savor it. I won't be spending my hard-earned money on that shit again for you for quite some time. Consider that your birthday present, Christmas present next year and a host gift for the next ten years."

Riley lifted his chin at the bartender. "He'll have a rye and tonic, lots of ice. Lime."

Emmett and Riley had been friends for nearly a decade. Four of them—Will Colson, Mark Herron, Riley McMillan and Emmett—had all gone to med school together, then they ended up at the same Seattle hospital. They were best friends, and even though their alcohol preferences varied, each man made sure to always have the others' preferred libation on hand. And Riley knew what Emmett drank, so he always kept both rye and tonic on hand just for Emmett. Riley himself only drank very expensive scotch, very expensive red wine and, for some weird reason, Pabst Blue Ribbon beer. He had a taste for the finer things in life, except when it came to beer. His buddy was a strange one, for sure.

Everything else in Riley and Daisy's world was top-of-the-line, though. They had become accustomed to a certain way of life and made no apologies for their expensive tastes. They were, however, also two of the most generous people Emmett had ever met.

Emmett thanked the bartender for his drink and took a sip. Fuck, that shit was good.

They turned around and stood with their backs to the bar,

surveying the living room full of people. There were more people in the kitchen where the food was set up and probably even more tucked away for private conversations—or whatever—in one of the dozen or so rooms of the house.

"So, see anybody you might like to get to know a bit better?" Riley asked, elbowing Emmett before he lifted his other arm and took a sip from his short, stocky tumbler of scotch on ice.

Emmett let his gaze circle the living room.

Everybody was dressed to impress.

However, he wasn't impressed.

The women were all gorgeous, but there wasn't anybody he would cross the street to say hello to.

His mind immediately went back to Zara and her piercing blue eyes, her quick wit, her show-stopping smile, those lush curves. Yeah, he'd cross the street to say hello to her. He'd probably run through the middle of traffic to say hello to her.

The doorbell chimed.

Riley's eyebrows waggled on his forehead. "Maybe that's Miss Right, right now."

Emmett rolled his eyes and took a sip of his rye.

Yeah, right.

There was no Miss Right for him. Not anymore.

Don't shy away from love simply because your heart is broken. Don't waste the best years of your life angry at what was, and instead spend those years searching and hoping for what could be.

Zara's words from earlier came back to him. She still had so much hope inside her. She still believed in a happily ever after, that there was a soul mate out there for everyone. Her heart was kind and full and open.

Emmett's heart had been ripped out and stomped on. Then what was left of it, battered and bruised and scarred beyond all recognition, had been locked shut—except for his daughter, who held the only key. He only wished he still had even an ounce of Zara's positivity and optimism. She was a breath of fresh air that smelled like the best and most beautiful flowers money could buy. Too bad he just wasn't convinced all that soul mate shit was for him anymore. Not after Tiff and the divorce from hell. Not after the way his ex— who he thought had been the perfect woman, his soul mate —had put him through the wringer.

Yeah, that whole soul mate thing was a fucking pipe dream.

Shit, he was starting to sound like Liam.

But as much as he quickly grew tired of his friend's anti-love tirades, Liam wasn't entirely wrong.

Emmett no longer believed in happily ever after, either. At least for him.

Nope. Wasn't going to happen. Wasn't in the cards.

But what he did believe in was his daughter. Wholeheartedly. That was it.

She was his soul mate.

Her soul was his to protect.

Josephine Eliza Strong was his heart, his soul, his everything. Nobody else.

And he didn't need anybody else. Work and JoJo kept him busy enough. He didn't need to add in the complications and demands of a relationship, of a woman.

And even if there was a Miss Right out there for him, she was probably with someone else or at another party. That seemed to be his luck these days. Yeah, Emmett had given up on finding a new person to share his life with, a soul mate. He just needed to put his head down, focus on work and focus on his daughter.

Love was complicated.

Love was overrated.

Love was not for him.

4

"I FORGOT ZIGGY!" Nolan exclaimed, turning back toward Zara's SUV and waiting for her to unlock it.

Zara exhaled, watching as her warm breath disappeared up into the cloudy sky. She shivered where she stopped, then pressed the fob to unlock her white Honda Pilot when Nolan was close enough to open the door himself.

Even though they lived just a couple of blocks away in their townhouse and could have walked, it was wintertime, and the sidewalks were icy. The last thing she needed was for her or her kid to slip and fall in the dark on their way home on New Year's Eve.

She waited on the sidewalk and pulled her winter coat up around her neck to shut out the chilly breeze. "Walking, please," she said in her best motherly tone. "You don't want to slip."

Nolan slowed his pace, but his mouth was still set in a thin, determined line, his dark brows furrowed in concentration. Moments later he caught up to his mother, his favorite stuffed animal, Ziggy the giraffe, now safely tucked in his arm.

"Can't ring in the new year without my best friend," Nolan said, slipping his hand into Zara's.

"Of course not," she said blithely.

She'd been just like Nolan when she was a child, heavily attached to her stuffed bear Arabella Blossom von Bearson. Now Arabella sat on a shelf in the flower shop, wearing a dress made out of Zara's grandmother's old apron. She was the shop mascot and a good luck charm. And although Zara knew she should probably take Arabella home and give her a good wash, she was reluctant to move her in case her absence caused the place to catch fire or a sudden sinkhole to emerge and swallow the shop whole. A dusty good luck charm was better than no good luck charm—that was how she looked at it, anyway.

The party house came into view, the street lined all the way along with cars. The steep driveway was packed too. Good thing she'd parked where she did. They started to make their way up the long slope.

"You think there will be other kids here?" Nolan asked.

Zara lifted a shoulder. "I think so. Mrs. McMillan told me this was a kid-friendly party. She told me her kids are going to be here."

Nolan smiled. "I hope so. Adults are boring."

Zara rolled her eyes and grinned down at her son. "Thanks, honey. Love you too." She lifted her fist to rap her knuckles against the door, but it swung open before she could even make one tap.

Daisy grinned at her, her green eyes sparkling. "You made it!"

Zara matched her smile and led Nolan in over the threshold, both of their eyes going wide as they took in the expanse of the beautifully decorated foyer. Garland was wrapped around the banister with big red velvet bows hanging ever three spindles. A beautiful spray of white twigs with little lights attached sat in the corner by a coat closet with small gold and red ornaments dangling from each twig end.

The whole house—at least from what Zara could see so far—was impeccably decorated, with not only good taste used to adorn the walls and valances but money as well.

"I'm so glad you came," Daisy went on, leading them inside from the cold and closing the door behind them.

"Well, when your best customer invites you to a party, you dare not say no. Your bi-weekly bouquet subscription is part of the reason why I can now afford to send Nolan to space camp in the summer."

Daisy tittered behind Zara as she helped Zara out of her coat. "I do love my flowers."

Zara turned back around and faced Daisy, holding out a box of chocolates. "I come bearing gifts. From that new chocolate place around the corner from my shop."

"Wicked Sister Chocolates?" Daisy's eyes went wide and her nostrils flared like she'd just caught the scent of a chai caramel bonbon. Zara had bought a dozen of those delectable morsels for herself that morning, nibbling away on them over the afternoon then practically sobbing when she reached into the box for another one only to discover she'd eaten them all.

Sometimes the world was unnecessarily cruel.

The memory of those bonbons made her mouth flood with saliva. "Have you been?"

Daisy shook her head as she accepted the wrapped box. "No, but I've heard a ton about her. People are just raving about her chocolates. And her London Fog petit gâteau has made the news. I tried to get her to do a platter or something for the party, but she was slammed and had to turn me down." She pouted but then smiled again. "I can't wait to try these. Thank you." Her eyes slid up the stairs. "I might have to hide them from Riley and the kids though."

Zara grinned, her hand falling to Nolan's back. "This is Nolan. He's hoping there are other kids around."

"Hi, Nolan!" Daisy chirped. "It's so nice to finally meet you. Your mom has told me so much about you."

Nolan nibbled on his bottom lip and clutched Ziggy even tighter to his chest.

"Can I hang up your coat for you?" Daisy asked, wandering around behind him.

He nodded.

Daisy helped Nolan out of his coat and hung it up in the closet with Zara's. "There are *loads* of other kids here. They're all downstairs, where we have a foosball table, a movie on, lots of games, coloring, puzzles, cookie decorating. You name it. There's also a babysitter and lots of food."

Nolan's eyes gleamed, and Zara chuckled. "I think you've won him over with the mention of cookie decorating. This kid loves to bake."

"Me too," Daisy said, her grin wide. Then her eyes fell to Zara's hand and her smile fell. She reached for it, concern clouding her moss-green eyes. "What happened to your hand? You okay?"

Zara continued to chuckle and made a face to convey her klutziness. "I forgot about that. Yeah, I'm fine. Was trying to do too much at once and ended up breaking a vase. Cut my hand pretty badly. Had to go to the ER and get it stitched up."

Daisy gently let go of Zara's hand, her mouth dipping into a frown, then a wince. "Yikes! Well, I hope that it was at least a hot doctor who stitched you up. Oh, and speaking of flowers earlier, you should see the bouquet Riley's friend brought me—ranunculus and peonies, my favorites. I think they were from your shop too. I recognized the wrapping."

Ranunculus and peonies?

It couldn't be, could it?

She hadn't done up any other bouquets like that all day.

What were the odds?

Heat wormed its way into Zara's cheeks and down her neck at the thought of the handsome Dr. Strong being at the party. How did he know Daisy and her husband?

Laughter at the top of the stairs drew their attention. Zara's mouth dropped open. The tall, dark-haired man turned around, and his mouth dropped open too before sliding up into a devilishly handsome smile.

"Ms. Olsen," he said, his amber eyes glittering with mischief in the ornate light that hung at the top of the staircase.

"Officer Astronaut Dr. Strong," she replied, flashing her own flirty smile.

Daisy and the tall blond man Emmett had been speaking to exchanged confused glances, but Zara barely paid attention.

"Come on, Nolan," Daisy said. "Let me show you to the kids' room downstairs."

Zara felt Nolan's back slip out from beneath her hand, and she began to ascend the stairs toward Emmett.

"You two know each other?" the blond man with the baby face asked, his gaze bouncing back and forth between Zara and the deliciously dressed Emmett.

Dark gray dress pants, a black button-down dress shirt opened just three buttons at the collar, and a shiny black leather belt. The man looked relaxed and drool-worthy.

His eyes remained glued to her as she climbed the stairs, his smile wicked and gloriously sexy. "We just met today, but what a meeting. Three times in one day, actually. And now four."

"Are the fates telling us something, Dr. Strong?" she asked, her belly doing flippity-flops the closer she got to him and his scrumptious smell and powerful height and frame.

"I'm not sure I believe in *fate*," he said, his mouth still smiling in a way that made her lady parts tingle and her nipples bead beneath her little black dress. "But I do believe that a chance meeting is one thing, but meeting someone four times in a single day makes one of them a stalker. And I'll already tell you, it isn't me." She wasn't sure how it was possible, but his grin grew even wider, causing the corners of his eyes to crinkle and his cheeks to apple and grow just a touch rosy.

Oh, he was a charmer. He held a drink in his hand, and by the way he was letting his eyes climb her body, she'd bet that was not his first drink.

She'd spent the better part of one evening last week going through her closet to find something to wear to the party. Nothing she found was worthy of a swanky New Year's Eve party though, and she ended up calling Michael and Shane in a tizzy asking for their help.

Thankfully, her best friend and his husband *loved* fashion and shopping, while Zara despised it. They took her shopping the very next day, and between the three of them, they—well, really just Michael and Shane—found Zara the perfect little black dress. It was flirty and feminine, sexy and sleek, showing off her best assets—her booty, her hips, her narrow waist and her breasts. Though she argued that her breasts—after nursing Nolan for two years—were not what they once were, but Michael and Shane said they were still rocking.

Who was she to argue with two gay men about the attractiveness of her breasts?

Zara reached the top of the stairs, and Emmett took a step back to give her room, his eyes continuing to appreciate her expensive boutique purchase.

A throat cleared beside them, and a body in a royal blue dress shirt came into her line of vision. "Riley McMillan," the man said, thrusting his hand toward Zara. "Daisy's husband and Emmett's co-worker and best friend."

Ah, so *that's* how Emmett knew Daisy. He worked with her husband. And here Zara was simply Daisy's florist.

Emmett rolled his eyes before taking a sip of the drink in his short glass tumbler. "*Dr.* McMillan is just a lowly surgeon though. Not a police officer astronaut doctor like me."

Zara snorted a laugh, continuing to admire the slight wrinkles at the corners of Emmett's amber eyes as he joked around and teased his friend. "Poor lowly Dr. McMillan," she added, knowing she needed to pay more attention to her host but unable to truly peel her eyes away from Emmett.

Riley's nose wrinkled, and one blond eyebrow lifted on his forehead. "What the hell are you two talking about?"

Emmett's hand fell to the small of Zara's back, and he encouraged her to move forward, away from the top of the stairs. "Inside joke, buddy. Don't worry your pretty little head about it." He glanced down at Zara. "Drink?"

Butterflies beat their wings double time in her belly at his intimate touch on her back. "You buying?"

His chuckle was deep and raspy. "Dr. McMillan is buying, which is even better." He led her through the living room full of handsomely dressed party people and into the dining room, where a tuxedo-clad bartender was busy stirring a beautiful glass pitcher with a rich red liquid inside, what appeared to be orange slices and cranberries.

"Tonight's signature drink is a mulled cranberry and clementine sangria," the bartender said. He removed the long metal spoon and the lifted the pitcher, tipping it up and filling four lined-up sugar-rimmed glasses.

Zara swallowed, then licked her lips. That sounded deadly.

She glanced at Emmett. It didn't look like he had one of the evening's signature drinks. His tumbler was too short and stocky, and the liquid appeared clear. "What are you drinking?" she asked.

"Rye and tonic," he replied. "It's one of the few things I can drink to excess and not be hung over the next day."

Her eyes went wide. "Planning to tie one on tonight, are you?"

That roguish glint was back in his eyes. "I hadn't been planning on it, no, actually hadn't been looking forward to the evening at all, but now that you're here, perhaps this party won't be all bad."

She felt the exact same way.

Zara bit her lip and glanced down at the now full and beautifully garnished short-stemmed sangria goblet the bartender was offering her. She grabbed it and immediately brought the rim to her lips, enjoying the jolt of sweetness that hit her tongue.

"May I have everyone's attention, please." Daisy's voice brought the murmuring to an abrupt end, and somewhere someone turned down the music. Emmett and Zara turned to find Daisy and Riley standing in the middle of their sunken living room in front off the enormous stone hearth, still decorated for Christmas. "Thank you all for coming tonight. We're so happy you could make it."

Daisy, as always, was dressed to stop traffic. A tight gold bandage-style dress showed off her incredible figure, and dark, professionally done smoky eye shadow played up her grass-green eyes. She was a showstopper for sure—and most likely without even trying. The woman just had that look. Freckles, bright eyes, a big smile, strawberry-blonde hair. She was a naturally beautiful woman. And the man beside her was just as comely. They were a striking duo, no doubt about it.

Zara's temperature ratcheted up several degrees as Emmett inched closer to her when someone passed by him. He didn't retreat from her side once the person had moved on.

She took a long sip of her icy drink, hoping it cooled her down.

It didn't work.

"As you can probably guess," Daisy continued, "given the nature of my profession, I am always looking to find new ways to help people find love. To find a connection."

Groans and sharp inhales filled the room.

Daisy was all smiles. "You guessed it, yes. This is a matchmaking party."

Zara's eyes flew up to Emmett's face. He glanced down at her, a smirk on his lips. "You didn't know?" he asked. "Remember I said that was the nature of the party I was attending tonight?"

She shook her head and whispered, "I only know Daisy from work. She's a client—a very *good* client, but a client. She invited me to the party last week. All we ever talk about are kids and flowers. I had no idea she was a matchmaker or that this was a matchmaking party. I never put two and two together when I recognized you." Her eyes narrowed.

She hadn't connected the dots because she'd been too busy thinking dirty thoughts for the future and what she'd like to do with him, rather than focusing on their past conversations.

He nodded as he took a sip of his drink. "I figured it out pretty quick. Daisy is always looking for a way to set people up. She's gone to some rather crazy lengths. Like abandoning six people in a snowy cabin in the mountains for a week." He snorted and shook his head. "That woman needs a hobby."

Zara's eyes went wide. "She just left them?"

He shrugged. "It was a luxury cabin with all the amenities. I don't think they were that hard up."

Zara's mind raced. She had no idea Daisy was a matchmaker. Had this been Daisy's angle all along? Befriend Zara only to eventually make her a client?

Did Daisy have someone specific in mind for Zara? Was he at the party?

Was he Emmett?

Or was it some other man entirely and she was standing here wasting her time flirting with Emmett when her soul mate was milling around the room chatting up all the other women?

"She's doing this pro bono," Emmett whispered. "She would never charge us for tonight, if that's what you're wondering. Yes, she makes *good, good* money doing what she does, but it's also a passion for her. So she does this a lot." He made a guttural noise in his throat. "Riley technically doesn't even have to work, Daisy makes such good coin."

Zara's mouth dropped open. Who'd have thought?

Emmett nodded. "Yeah, she's that good."

Heat filled her cheeks. Was her soul mate somewhere in that house? Or was it more of a singles can mingle kind of thing? Not that she was interested in mingling with anybody but the sexy officer-astronaut-doctor who was currently brushing his elbow against hers as someone else pushed past him, but she had to wonder if she was making a mistake chatting him up when she should be chatting up everyone to see if there was a greater connection out there.

"Mingle, chat, connect," Daisy went on. "There are no expectations tonight. Unlike some of my other matchmaking schemes"—her smile grew just a touch wicked—"I have not made sure your exact match is here. Some of you may find love, some of you may not. I have simply made sure that besides Riley and myself, all of our guests are single. I also made sure any of you with children were not excluded, and you can head downstairs to check on your wee ones at any point in time." She wrapped her arm around her husband's waist. "Please, enjoy the food, the drinks and the company, and may this new year be your best year yet!"

The room erupted into applause, though Zara struggled to put any real pep into her clap. That might have been because she was too concerned with spilling her drink, but there was also a frisson of unease that coursed through her. She'd never been set up before. Never been on a blind date. How did it work?

She drained her drink.

Emmett's warm and hearty chuckle beside her had her shifting her eyes up to his smiling face. "Another one?" he asked. "Not a fan of being ambushed?" He took her empty glass from her and walked away toward the bar, moments later returning with a fresh glass with the same drink as before, his hand once again falling to the small of her back. As if attracted by magnets or something. As if it belonged there.

Maybe it did.

It certainly felt right.

"I'm just not a fan of the unexpected," she said, immediately taking another sip. Liquid courage. She needed it. "You're not upset about being ambushed?"

"I was. Riley read me the riot act earlier, told me not to ruin his wife's party. Hence why I was in your shop earlier buying flowers for Miss Daisy. A peace offering."

Well, at least she wasn't the only one suddenly feeling like a broodmare about to be led up onto the auction block with a stable full of stallions whinnying behind her. Not that she could remember the last time she'd made a stallion whinny —or a man took a second glance.

Not at forty-four anyway. Her head-turning days were behind her.

He leaned down next to her ear. "If it gets to be too much of a meat market, we can always head downstairs and party with the kids. I saw the spread Daisy's got for them down there." He frowned and nodded as though he approved. "I'm not above grilled cheese and veggies with dip."

Tension fled her shoulders; she smiled. "Neither am I."

His eyes twinkled. "So, Zara *Brilliant*," he started, grinning down at her, his hand still around her waist, "tell me about yourself. Have you always been a florist?"

She took another sip of her drink. "I have, actually. I'm a third-generation florist. My grandmother owned the shop. She passed it down to my mother, and she passed it down to me."

His grin grew wider. "That's really cool. I'm a third-generation doctor."

A hot third-generation doctor.

She slid her tongue along her bottom lip, tasting the sugar from the rim of her glass. Emmett's eyes grew wide, and the coppery color around his pupils seemed to glow.

"And Zara, where does that name come from?" he asked, keeping the conversation going, despite the pheromones that seemed to be ricocheting back and forth between them. Her temperature spiked. She took another sip of her icy drink. Like before, it did nothing to cool her off.

She swallowed before answering. "My grandmother was Italian, my grandfather Egyptian, my mother a combination of the two, and my father is of Scandinavian descent. Hence *Ols-son* or *Olsen*. My mother's paternal grandmother was named Zara, and the two were very close, so she named me after her."

"It's a lovely name," he purred, his voice like a zephyr in her ear that made her nipples instantly harden and desire sizzle in her veins.

She licked her lips again. "Thank you. It's often pronounced wrong, and it used to bug me when people would call me *Zair-ah,* rather than *Zar-rah*, but now I just answer to both. Life's too short to get upset about that kind of crap."

His chuckle swept across her skin like a warm breeze, and he squeezed her hip. "That's one way to look at it. I never really thought to pronounce it any other way besides the right way. But then again, you introduced yourself as *Zar-rah*, so ... "

A big shadow blocked out some of the light from overhead, and suddenly two men approached Emmett from behind, one of them slapping him on the back.

"Hey, thought we might find you here," the older-looking of the two men said, a boxy tumbler of amber liquid clutched tightly in his big hand.

Emmett's smile grew and he turned around, releasing his grip on her hip and shaking hands with two very handsome, very similar looking men. "Hey, Daisy roped you two into her party too, did she?"

The younger-looking man shrugged. "I think I might be ready to enter the dating pool again. Besides, the food is amazing and the booze is free." He popped what looked to be a canape covered in salmon and cucumber into his mouth. "Mason should be here eventually, too. Think he's running late though, tying up loose ends at the bar. Big private party there tonight."

Emmett's hand fell back to the small of Zara's back, practically singeing her skin beneath her dress with his heat. "Sorry, I'm being rude. Zara, these are my friends Liam and his brother Scott."

Liam, the older-looking one, thrust his free hand forward. "Nice to meet you, Zara." His eyes flicked back up to Emmett. "You work fast. Didn't think you were ready to start dating. Thought you were anti-love, anti-commitment like me." He glanced down at the very expensive watch on his wrist. "I'd say you won this party. Ain't nobody in here already hooked up besides you two."

Anti-love? Anti-commitment?

Had he said all of that to her earlier? She couldn't remember. She'd just gone off on her tangent of optimism, telling him to embrace the future and hope and *blah blah blah*. Here she thought she was being clever and witty giving him her VIP sage advice, but had she really been speaking to a brick wall?

She just thought he was gun-shy from a bad divorce, but was he really taking himself off the market completely? Was he giving up on finding his happily ever after forever?

Emmett made a noise in his throat and shuffled twice on his feet. "We met earlier today, just ran into each other here." He glanced down at Zara and winked. "She's actually stalking me. I'm considering filing for a restraining order. She's probably hatching a plot to make a doll out of my hair as we speak." His fingers tightened around her waist, and her hip knocked his.

Heat pooled in her belly.

Liam laughed, and Scott, the younger-looking man with the slightly crooked nose, grinned at Zara, his dark brown eyes slowly, *very* slowly running up the length of her. "So you're still available? I'm okay with a stalker as long as they don't try to kill me. Nothing wrong with being somebody's obsession. Worked out for Zak and Aurora, didn't it? Zak texted Liam to say she's at his place for the night." He shrugged. "Besides, it would be a step up from what I was with my ex—an afterthought." Anger glimmered for just a fraction of a second in his eyes. Anger *and* hurt.

Emmett took a half step closer to her, and his fingers now bunched in the fabric of her dress.

Zara's body blazed in a full-on inferno now.

"Nope, she's not available" Liam chuckled. There was no

mistaking the teasing glint in his dark brown eyes—the same shade as his brother's. His mouth turned up into a far too mischievous smile and he started singing the tune to Queen's "Another One Bites the Dust" before his snicker quickly turned into a full-blown laugh, his head tossed back and his mouth open and everything.

Emmett reached out with his free hand and lightly shoved Liam in the shoulder. "You're an ass."

Liam seemed completely unfazed. "Perhaps. I prefer to call myself a realist, though. You guys are dropping like flies."

What was he talking about?

Dropping like flies?

Liam must have noticed the puzzled expression on Zara's face, so he decided to take pity on her. "See, we're part of a little club I formed."

Little club? Like an anti-love club? Anti-woman's club? Divorced and jaded men's club?

"We're The Single Dads of Seattle," Scott added. "Just a bunch of single fathers who play poker every Saturday night."

Oh.

"But we're more than that," Liam replied, his shoulders going back and his strong chin lifting. "We're a support group. A support group that *I* started, after I saw far too many fathers being treated unfairly during divorce procedures and custody battles. I'm a divorce lawyer and single father myself."

Oh!

"We're a minority, you know," he went on.

Huh?

Zara had to keep herself from laughing. A privileged rich, white man calling himself a *minority* was about one of the most laughable things she'd ever heard. But she remained quiet and let him finish.

"There are tons of resources and support groups for single moms but nothing really for single dads. Particularly those dads that have either full custody or shared custody. Even in a big city like Seattle, single dads are overlooked and underrepresented."

Oh, *that* kind of a minority.

"I wanted to change that. There are single dads out there who are more than just weekend parents. They need a place where they can feel supported."

Scott slapped his brother on the back. "And that's exactly what Liam did. It's a brotherhood of sorts. We watch each other's kids, give advice, knock some sense into each other. Pick up each other's kids from school if needed. A village." Scott flexed his arms and grinned. "A *manly* village."

Zara snorted through her nose. She liked Scott. He was funny and a charmer without being a bit of a sarcastic ass like Liam.

"Only a bunch of them are finding women … " Liam went on, adding a big sarcastic eye roll. Surprise, surprise.

"So you kicked them out?" Zara asked, unsure whether she should admire Liam or move away from him.

He shook his head. "No. Of course not. But their buy-in for poker doubles as soon as they're in a relationship." He tossed his head back and laughed again. This guy really thought he was hilarious. "I'm making a killing at the poker table. These love-drunk suckers are too caught up with their women to pay attention to their cards. I'm on a serious winning streak."

Zara rolled her eyes. Okay, so Liam wasn't a complete jerk. Just a hurt jerk who simultaneously exploited and supported his friends. His heart was in the right place, though.

Having been through her own messy divorce, she couldn't blame his ire. Thankfully, she and Marcello hadn't had children they needed to fight for custody over. And she never could have asked for a better co-parent than Michael.

"Where's Richelle tonight? I wouldn't exactly call you *single*," Emmett countered, frustration beginning to radiate off him in heated waves.

Zara wasn't so sure she wanted his arm wrapped around her anymore. She didn't like the tension in his neck or jaw, didn't like the way he'd shoved his friend in the shoulder earlier, despite how much Liam may have deserved it.

Liam made a dismissive face. "That's not the nature of our *arrangement*. It's casual. Richelle can date other guys if she wants. Not that she does, as far as I know."

"So you don't even know where your woman is tonight?" Emmett asked, his tone taking on an edge that Zara couldn't altogether place but knew she didn't like. She'd always had a keen ability to sense someone's energy, and right now she was picking up on a lot of negative energy surrounding the man whose hand was bunched at the hip of her dress.

Unlike Liam, whose demeanor still seemed carefree and jovial, despite his anti-love rhetoric, Emmett seemed legitimately angry and almost spiteful.

It was New Year's Eve. She didn't need to be around angry and spiteful. She needed to be around happy and hopeful.

As much as her ex-husband had hurt her, she still had hope that her soul mate was out there, that love was out there.

She shook herself free of his grasp and took a half step to the side away from him.

Emmett's gaze flashed from Liam to her. Confusion colored his cheeks and flared in the intense amber of his eyes. His jaw flexed.

"I know where Richelle *is*," Liam continued, seeming to be either oblivious to what was passing between Emmett and

Zara or not caring. "She's at home with her kid. I'll see her on Wednesday night for sexy time like I always do."

Scott snorted next to him and shook his head. "You're kidding yourself if you don't think you have feelings for her."

Emmett's eyes burned into Zara, a thousand questions firing at her all at once without a word fleeing from his lips.

"I'm hungry," Liam said blandly. "Did Paige cater this thing?"

"Yeah, I think Mitch said something about her providing food for Daisy's party," Scott replied.

"Well, fuck, then I *really* need to load up my plate before it's all gone." A hand landed on Emmett's shoulder once again. "Catch up with you again later, buddy," Liam said, the tone of his voice filled with amusement. "Nice to meet you, Zara. I'm sure we'll be seeing *a lot* more of you in the future." He started humming "Another One Bites the Dust" again as he made his exit.

"You're an ass," Scott said to his brother, offering Zara an apologetic look before he followed his big brother off in the direction of the buffet.

"An ass with a great ass," Liam retorted over his shoulder, before they both disappeared into another room.

Emmett's fingers wrapped around her elbow. "I'm sorry about that. Liam can be a jerk. He's got a big heart—but an even bigger mouth."

It wasn't Liam she was disenchanted with though. Liam still had a smile on his face. Emmett did not.

Her mouth grew tight, and she nodded once, stepping out of his grasp once again. "It's fine." She scanned the room for Daisy, finding her host off in the far corner of the living room, deep in conversation with a very attractive redheaded woman. "I have to go talk to Daisy. Will you excuse me?"

Before she could rethink her decision or let him convince her otherwise, she stepped away from him, his wonderfully manly smell and the heat of his big frame. Her head hurt from that information overload from Liam and Scott. It also hurt at the idea of Emmett being anti-love and anti-commitment. Was he just looking for a casual hookup like Liam? A fuck-buddy? A friend with benefits like Liam?

She was too old for that shit.

She was also too old to deal with someone with anger issues, and she was beginning to wonder if Emmett had some. Even though she didn't have any fancy diplomas hanging on the living room wall of her townhouse, she considered herself a PhD-worthy graduate of the school of hard knocks and a keen observer of people. She could tell the intention and mood of a person who walked into her flower shop before they even made it to the front counter. She was also very, very good at picking out or designing the absolute perfect bouquet or arrangement for a person by asking them only three simple questions. One: Where is your ideal vacation? Two: Top quality you look for in a good friend or partner? And three: If you could sit down with any person from your past and ask them one question, who would it be and what would you ask them?

From those three (well, technically four) questions she could discern so much about that person and put together the ideal flower arrangement for them. It was an uncanny ability her mother had passed down to her, and her mother had passed down to her. She was a third-generation florist, after all. Flowers and making people happy with her beautiful arrangements were in her blood. She eat, slept and breathed buds, blooms and bouquets.

And even though she hadn't asked Emmett any of those questions, she could read him like an open book, and she wasn't sure she was entirely into the page she'd landed on.

However, she also wasn't entirely convinced he was a book she was willing to put down and walk away from yet either. Perhaps just bookmark it for later? Would there be a later?

With even more confusing thoughts cannoning around her head, she made to go down the stairs into the sunken living room when a hand grabbed hers and caused her to turn around again.

It was Emmett. His eyes held a pleading look that made her second-guess her decision to walk away. Made her second-guess the bookmark and instead consider diving in deep and reading him from the first chapter to the last.

"Come find me," he said, hope coloring his voice, "please. I want to get to know you better." Then he let her go, winked and headed into the kitchen, leaving Zara standing on the steps, her heart thundering in her ears, her nipples achingly hard beneath her dress and her panties suddenly very damp.

5

EMMETT NEEDED TO FIND LIAM. He needed to give his *friend* a piece of his mind—and then some. He'd gone and scared off Zara with his talk of anti-love and anti-commitment, lumping Emmett into Liam's blackhearted fold.

Emmett wasn't *anti*-love, per se. He just didn't believe in happily ever after or soul mates anymore. But love? Sure.

Maybe.

His heart wasn't black. Maybe just a dark shade of gray?

He could certainly see himself wanting to spend more time with Zara. Get to know her, see if the fallacy of happily ever after wasn't a fallacy at all but, in fact, a true-blue possibility.

He was getting ahead of himself though. He'd only just met the woman, for Christ's sake. Was this how the other single dads felt when they met a woman they wanted to see more of, after their marriages ended or were through their grieving periods? Was this how Mark felt when he met Tori? Like he needed to be around her, spend time with her, get to know her. Had it consumed him? Because it certainly felt like it was beginning to consume Emmett, and it hadn't even been twenty-four hours. Hell, it hadn't even been twelve hours since he met the woman, and yet he couldn't get her out of his head.

His mind swam with conflicting thoughts. Thoughts about Zara, thoughts about Tiff and their horribly messy divorce. Thoughts about JoJo and what it would mean introducing somebody new into her world. Tiff had gone about introducing JoJo to Huntley all wrong, and his daughter now hated the man. Emmett could never do that to his little girl, never.

Stupid Liam getting into his head.

Liam could be a jerk.

He stopped at the bar and grabbed another drink before heading toward the kitchen in search of his friend and club founder. Sure enough, there was Liam stuffing his face while talking up a cute blonde in a *very* short black dress. Zara's black dress had been sexier. It left more to the imagination and played up all her incredible, grabbable assets. This woman was pretty, but she was too lean, and Emmett liked his woman to have a little something he could hold on to. Plus, this chick's laugh was atrocious. If that was her real laugh, anyway. God, how he hoped it wasn't real. She was tossing her wavy locks over her shoulder and tittering like a little bird.

Liam wasn't *that* funny. He was, however, one of Seattle's most eligible bachelors.

The man was well-off, well-connected and a socialite. Liam knew everybody, or so it seemed. Because no matter where Emmett went with Liam Dixon, the man ran into somebody he knew, somebody he'd either gone to school with or knew through someone else.

He was also quick on his feet, smart as fuck and still had

all his hair. So did Emmett, thank God. He would *not* look good bald.

But really, what woman with two working ovaries and no ring on her finger wouldn't take a stab at landing Liam Dixon?

Liam knew it though. If there was one thing at which Liam was a savant, it was reading people. The man was a shark and could smell blood, deceit and phoniness over a mile away.

Only Emmett wouldn't necessarily call what this poor woman was up to deceit or phoniness. She was simply out for her happily ever after. Her clock was ticking—and probably quite loudly—and she was going to take advantage of Daisy's party, hoping her Prince Charming would be a high-powered Seattle divorce attorney who made over six figures.

She was barking up the wrong tree, unfortunately. Everything was true, except for the happily ever after. She'd never get that with Liam Dixon, the Born-Again Bachelor, as they called him.

Emmett needed to help her realize that before she wasted any more of her time.

"There you are," Emmett said, sidling up next to the woman whose lashes were so long it looked as though a million-legged spider was repeatedly attacking her face as she blinked. "Thought I'd find you here with food in your mouth." He offered the woman his hand. "Emmett Strong. You know who this is, right?" he asked, tilting his head toward Liam.

She nodded, hunger glimmering in her eyes. "Mhmm."

"Then you know he's a bachelor for life. You're wasting your time."

The woman's nude-painted lips dropped open. So did Liam's.

Emmett grinned at his buddy. "Right? You said so yourself just a moment ago that love doesn't exist and you don't do commitment anymore."

Emmett heard Scott snort a laugh behind him. He was busy chatting up a cute brunette in a dark green pantsuit but no shirt—or bra—beneath it.

Liam's face went the same color as the cherry tomato on his plate. He swallowed the food in his mouth. "I, uh ... "

Emmett cocked his head to the side, waiting for Liam to dig himself out of the hole he'd dug for not only himself, but for Emmett as well.

The blonde's dark gray eyes swiveled back and forth between Liam and Emmett. "I, uh ... I'm going to go. I'm *not* anti-love or anti-commitment, and my clock is ticking far too loudly for me to waste my time trying to convert a cynic."

Called it.

She scanned Liam from toe to top, her mouth curling up into almost a snarl. "It's a damn shame." Then she spun on her five- or six- or whatever-inch heels and was gone. Literally seconds later, she was tossing her waves behind her again, laughing and resting her hand on the arm of one of the cardiologists from the fourth floor of the hospital. Oh, that woman was on the prowl.

"What the fuck, man?" Liam asked, taking a drink of his scotch. "She was into me. You could have cost me my kiss at midnight."

Emmett glared at Liam. He wasn't letting his friend off the hook, not yet. "In the words of Matt Damon, 'How you like them apples?' What the fuck, dude? You don't say that shit to a woman, particularly one you can tell I'm interested in. You went all high school shithead, flapping your gums about shit to Zara. She couldn't get out of there fast enough once you filled her head with the idea that I'm all anti-love and anti-commitment like you. Keep your fucking cynicism to yourself."

Liam's mouth dipped into a harsh frown, and he scratched the back of his neck. "Shit, sorry. I thought I was just, you know, joking around. Chatting."

"You *chat* about the weather or your favorite restaurant. You don't sabotage me." Emmett hadn't realized he'd been bunching his fists at his sides until a sharp pain sprinted up both forearms.

Scott wandered over. "Everything okay?" The brunette he'd been chatting with had linked her arm through his.

Liam glanced down at the woman but didn't really acknowledge her. He nodded. "Yeah, just getting a taste of my own medicine from the good doctor, I suppose."

Emmett huffed out a breath. "Well, not quite. Unless you were genuinely interested in that woman?"

Liam shook his head, his expression dismissive.

"Didn't think so."

"I'm sorry. I'll keep my opinions to myself. To be fair though, you do give off the whole anti-love vibe. Any of the guys would agree with me." Liam glanced at his brother for help.

Scott nodded. "You kind of do, dude."

"Do you want me to go talk to her?" For once in his forty-one-year-old life, Liam Dixon actually looked truly apologetic and remorseful.

Emmett shook his head and grunted. "You've done enough. I'll take care of it."

It took him over an hour to make it through the throng of people and back into the living room. Riley and Daisy's house was packed, and it looked like people were taking the whole free *matchmaking* thing pretty darn seriously.

The googly and fuck-me eyes Emmett walked through as he went on the search for Zara were enough to make him want to run home and shower. The pheromones in that house were thick and smothering.

When he finally spotted her, his blood began to boil. Like bubble up and froth to the point where he wasn't sure if steam was coming from his ears or not.

She was sitting on the edge of the love seat chatting with Felix de Beer, or should he say *Dr.* Felix de Beer, chief of orthopedic surgery at the hospital.

Fuck!

Felix was a decent enough guy, great surgeon. Had a bit of an ego, but what surgeon didn't? At least he wasn't a neuro-surgeon. Those guys' egos could be seen from another galaxy.

Originally from South Africa, Dr. de Beer had a smile that made the nurses blush and an accent that caused even the chief of surgery, a woman in her early sixties, to get a little flustered.

The women at the hospital even had a nickname for him that they thought they kept under wraps. They did not. Even Felix knew they called him Dr. de *Fine*. They compared his looks to that of Ryan Reynolds, only with a touch more salt and pepper and a bit more of a tan—but with an accent, which apparently was the icing on the man candy cake—or so said at least half a dozen nurses.

And Zara was talking to him.

Zara was laughing with him.

Zara was flirting with him.

Emmett grabbed a flute of champagne off the tray of a passing waiter and chugged it. His own drink was empty and long gone. He needed something to take the edge off, and quick. But the bubbles shot straight up his nose, and for a second there, he thought he might go blind.

By the time he opened his eyes, Felix de Beer's hand was dangerously close to touching Zara's knee, and the two were laughing once again.

Emmett saw red.

And that wasn't just because he was angry. A woman in a bright red dress had just stepped in front of him, her bosom practically heaving out of the deep V. "Hi, I'm Amanda." She stuck out her hand. "Are you a doctor too? Seems to be a lot of doctors here tonight."

She was pretty, Emmett wasn't going to deny that. Her smile was sweet, her makeup tasteful. She was probably on the upper end of thirty. He saw no ring on her finger, but there was a faint tan line where a ring had once been.

Hmmm ...

Divorced? Broken engagement? Widow?

Her hand was still out, waiting for him to take it.

He did. Because although he was inconspicuously trying to see around this Amanda woman to catch another glimpse of Zara and Felix, he wasn't an entirely rude asshole.

"So, are you a doctor?" she asked again, her handshake on the feebler side.

Zara's handshake had been strong.

He nodded. "Yeah, I am. I work with Riley. I'm in the ER." He angled his head to the side to try and see around Amanda's dark red hair. From the looks of it, Zara and Felix were still deep in whatever hilarious conversation they were having. His hand having moved even closer now to her knee.

Emmett wanted to chop off that hand.

"That's so cool," Amanda went on. "I'm a pharmaceutical rep. Daisy and I met in spin class."

Emmett nodded. "Mhmm ... "

Amanda moved to the side just enough that he could

finally see Zara. She was laughing—again. Fuck, she hadn't laughed that much with him. What was Felix telling her that was so goddamn side-splitting?

Suddenly, Zara's eyes flicked up from where she'd been staring at her lap—where the knuckles of Felix's hand gently brushed her bare knee from where he sat gripping the arms of his chair—and they lasered in on Emmett. Her smile immediately fled her lips, but her eyes held a heat that would set any house completely aflame. She also shifted where she sat so that Felix was no longer touching her.

Was she bored with Felix?

Emmett was bored with Amanda.

You're not even giving Amanda a chance. She's standing there talking to you, and you haven't heard a word she's said. You're being an asshole.

He stared back at Zara, then his eyes slid to the left, down the long hallway toward the bedrooms. Her eyes followed.

He lifted his eyebrows.

She lifted hers. Then nodded.

She nodded.

She. Nodded.

He reached out and placed his hands gently on either side of Amanda's slender arms. Her skin was cool to the touch, but he also didn't mistake the flare in her blue eyes or the shiver that caused her whole body to tremble.

"Amanda, right?"

She nodded hopefully.

"I'm really sorry. You seem like a really nice person, are absolutely gorgeous, and I'm sure you're going to find your Mr. Right here tonight, but I don't think he's me. Will you excuse me, please?" he asked, hoping he was being as polite as possible and not offending one of Daisy's guests.

He really didn't want to hurt this poor woman's feelings.

She was only looking for love. A hopeless romantic, unlike himself.

Not anymore, at least.

Though he had been, once.

Hopelessly in love, a romantic to his core, head over heels for the woman he thought was his forever partner.

He'd pulled out all the stops to propose to Tiff, spent a fortune on her ring, on the wedding, on their house. He never forgot a birthday, an anniversary. Bought her flowers just because. They had a standing date night once a week. He thought he was doing everything right, because she was his Miss Right.

And then she broke him. She broke them. Broke his heart. Broke their family.

Now he wasn't sure he had a romantic bone left in his body.

This poor woman standing in front of him with hope in her eyes and heart didn't need his hurt and jaded assholeness breaking her spirit.

Besides, he'd made Riley a promise he wouldn't ruin Daisy's party, wouldn't offend any of the guests. He intended to keep that promise.

He glanced back around Amanda's body to see Zara still chatting with Felix, but she'd shifted even further away from him and her posture seemed rigid and ready to flee. Was she making her clean getaway as well?

Emmett glanced back up at Amanda. Her face was sad.

Shit.

"I'm sorry," he said again, exhaling. "If you don't find Mr. Right tonight, let me know. I belong to a great club full of successful single guys, and I'm sure one of them would fall head over heels for you. I'd be happy to play matchmaker."

Her spirits seemed to brighten just a tad.

Phew.

He said his goodbye, then released her arms and stepped away, his eyes never leaving Zara as he headed down the hallway until she was no longer in sight.

He found one of the spare bedrooms the waitstaff had used to keep the crates of clean plates and glasses.

He stepped inside the room, sat down on the bed and waited.

6

WHAT WAS she doing heading down the hallway away from the party?

Getting away from boring Dr. de Beer, that was what.

And meeting up with Emmett.

She swallowed the nerves that had started to simmer in her belly and instead ran her hands down the black lace skirt of her dress, smoothing it out, but also wiping away the sweat from her palms.

Felix de Beer had been nice enough—and, boy oh boy, had he been handsome enough—but he was boring.

Zara couldn't remember the last time she'd faked a laugh so many times in the span of ten minutes.

Perhaps it had been at Michael and Shane's wedding when Shane's dimwitted brother got up and made a toast to the grooms. His humor had been off, not inappropriate, just not funny.

The voices in the living room faded the farther away from the crowd she got. Door upon door she passed. Sheesh, there were a lot of rooms in this house. Where was he? Had she read his eyes and brows wrong?

No, she couldn't have.

Wouldn't be the first time you misinterpreted somebody's body language though.

Yeah, but that ended up resulting in her and Shane's best friend Deacon bumping noses when she thought they were going in for a kiss, and he—who turned out to be gay—had thought they were going in for a hug. Awkward.

Thankfully they both laughed it off, and Deacon was now a close friend.

Had she read Emmett wrong too? Was he actually interested in that *other* woman?

Jealousy had licked up her spine the moment she saw that gorgeous redhead approach Emmett. That woman was by far the most attractive person at the party, and she'd lasered in on Emmett. And yet, he wanted to meet Zara. He wanted to talk to Zara.

She realized after taking a moment to cool off and speak with Daisy that Emmett was still reeling from his messy divorce. She'd picked Daisy's brain on the broody and intriguing doctor, so much so that her friend couldn't stop smiling or bouncing on her toes at the thought of Emmett and Zara getting together.

"He just seems like a bit of a hothead," Zara finally said, exhaling through her nose before she took a sip of her festive drink. The sangria was lethal, and she knew if she wasn't careful, she'd be stumbling home, dragging Nolan on his toboggan behind her.

"He can be," Daisy confirmed, nodding at a few guests that passed them. "But he's also one of the most loyal, honest and amazing men I know. He loved Tiff with all his heart, and she tore it clean out of his chest and stomped all over it. So if he comes across as a little jaded or hesitant, it's justified."

Zara ran her index finger over the rim of her glass, picking up some of the sugar, then popping her finger into her mouth. "Do you know if he's doing anything to help with the anger?"

"He works out a lot. He also goes to The Rage Room every now and then. Have you been?"

Zara shook her head. She hadn't yet, but Nolan had been itching to go. It was ages eight and up though, so he couldn't wait for his birthday in March. He wanted to have his party there. Nothing but a bunch of little boys smashing things with bats and hammers, followed by pizza and cake. What on earth could go wrong?

"He's a great guy, Zara, truly. I wouldn't have invited him if he wasn't. A tremendous father, genuine friend, wonderful doctor, and he'd been a devoted husband too."

Well, he certainly ticked all the right boxes.

But ...

"If you saw him get angry over something, particularly something ridiculous, call him out on it. Don't let him get away with behaving like an ass. Emmett can be a hardhead, but he's also not above growth. We've all seen it. He'll respect you more for not putting up with his shit than if he finds out you resent him without giving him a chance to either explain himself or change." Daisy took a sip of her champagne, her French manicure looking like a million bucks in combination with the enormous diamonds on her left ring finger as she cradled the flute of bubbly.

The woman had an inherent sophistication about her that Zara wished she had even five percent of.

Daisy's bright green eyes turned soft, a twinkle of something akin to hope flickering behind the flecks of gold around her pupil. "Challenge him. Emmett likes strong women who challenge him."

Challenge him.

Zara could do that.

She'd never backed down from a challenge in her life.

And if Dr. Emmett Strong was as wonderful as Daisy made him out to be, Zara would give him another shot, but not without setting a few things straight first.

Her pace picked up, her heels clicking on the wood floor as she continued down the hallway. Suddenly, she was hauled into a room by a warm, strong hand wrapped around her bicep.

She gasped, but that gasp was quickly captured by lips. Deliciously soft but strong and demanding lips.

A man's lips.

Emmett's lips.

Yes, please.

He pushed her back up against the wall and released her arm, cupping her face with both his hands and prying her lips apart with his tongue. She acquiesced and opened for him, welcoming him in and allowing him to deepen and control the kiss.

God, she'd missed kissing.

And what a man to break her dry spell with.

Emmett Strong could kiss.

Officer Astronaut Dr. Emmett Strong could *really* kiss.

She weaved the fingers of her good hand into his hair, tugging on the ends, and letting the short, silky curls slip across the insides of her digits. It tickled, sending shards of longing straight down to her core.

Her breasts tingled, and she could feel her nipples tighten.

She wasn't sure what she was expecting, following him down the hallway, but it hadn't been this. It hadn't been a spontaneous, passionate man whose knee was surreptitiously pushing her legs apart until her center rested on his thick, muscular thigh. She could feel his growing erection against her and fought the urge to feel him for herself.

He broke their kiss, and she sucked in a sharp breath as

his tongue followed the line of her throat and he sucked the hollow. Her eyes flashed open and fell to the still open door next to them.

Should she shut it?

Would that send a bigger message to everyone out in the living room than if they left it open?

Stop overthinking things and just enjoy the moment.

Right. The moment.

He dropped one hand from her face to the hem of her dress, and slowly, ever so fucking painfully slowly, his hand pushed beneath the hem and up and behind her until he cupped one cheek of her ass.

She wasn't wearing any pantyhose and had decided to feel sexy on the inside and out, slipping into a pair of black lacy boy shorts that only covered half of each cheek.

His fingers dug into one of those cheeks, causing a pleasurable pain to light like a flame inside her core. He rocked her against him, letting her clit rub over his thigh, the friction exquisite and driving her closer to the edge.

A rush of wetness flowed from her, and she was sure he would probably have a damp spot on his thigh when they were finished.

"Why'd you walk away from me?" he asked, pulling her tighter against him. Starbursts flashed behind her eyes as her now damp panties stroked her clit. "Don't tell me Liam scared you off." Warm, wet kisses made a path of fire along her collarbone and chest. "I'm not anti-anything, just wary."

"Have you been burned?" she asked, knowing the answer but wanting to hear it from him. She tugged harder on his hair until he groaned and took her mouth again. His tongue swept inside and tangoed with hers, drinking her in like a starved man lost at sea. Tasting her as if she were the most forbidden of fruit, but he was willing to risk it all for her.

He broke the kiss once again. "I have been burned," he

finally said. "Badly." His kisses became softer, covering her cheeks and nose, each eyelid. "I'm gun-shy and perhaps a bit jaded, but I'm not afraid to play with matches ... as long as the fire we start heats me up but doesn't smoke me out."

Her eyes flashed open wide. His gaze held her hostage. Magnetic, liquid pools of desire turned her insides to jelly and made her knees threaten to buckle.

"I hated seeing you talking to Felix," he whispered, trailing a finger gently down the side of her face, encircling her jaw and then cupping the back of her head. His fingers threaded into her hair, kneading her scalp, which only made her shut her eyes again from how incredible it felt. "Don't tell me you want to get back out there to him."

Her laugh was breathy and quiet. "You mean go hear more about his boat? I'm okay where I am, thanks."

He skimmed his lips along the sweep of her cheek, the puffs of air from his chuckle warm against her skin. "He does like to talk about that boat, doesn't he?"

She rolled her eyes and nodded. "One might think Dr. de Beer is overcompensating for something."

The smile that brushed her lips made her pussy clench and goosebumps break out over her bare arms. They were lip to lip now, but not kissing. Tasting the other's breath. "One might think." His tongue skimmed along her bottom lip. "I'll have you know I have absolutely *nothing* I need to overcompensate for. I don't even *have* a boat. Don't need one."

Zara moaned. "That's good to know." She tugged on his hair again. "Do you have a yard, though?"

He pulled away from her slightly and scrunched up his face in confusion. "A yard?"

She nodded, her eyelids still heavy. "Yeah, I love a man with a *nice, big yard.* One I can spend *all* my time in. Plant a garden, watch it grow. I'd spend *all* my free time in his yard if I could."

Emmett's eyes glimmered with amusement. "Oh, Zara *Brilliant* Baby, I will have you know my yard is *huge. Massive.* And you can spend as much time in it as you like." He shrugged. "Though it's not something I brag about. Just know, my yard *is* above average in size, and no woman has ever complained about its size. No woman has ever complained about it, period."

"Are we still talking about your yard?" she asked, chuckling.

His grin made her panties dampen even more. "We can talk about it all night if that's what you want." The hand that cupped her cheek angled her face up just slightly so she was forced to stare directly into his intense, mesmerizing amber eyes. "Spend the rest of the evening getting to know me. Don't let what my idiot friend said scare you. I'm not a complete lost cause. I just need the right person to make me see that the world isn't as fucked up as I think it is." He squeezed her butt and hiked her up against him.

There was no doubt about it. Emmett Strong wasn't overcompensating for a damn thing.

"And you think that person is me?" she asked, her chest rising and falling rapidly, her lips tingling from his kisses, her mind fuzzy from the pleasure.

His eyes flared. "I know it's you."

"I didn't like how you treated Liam. If he's just as jaded and hurt as you, you should be more compassionate." As much as she wanted to keep kissing and continue on down the path they were on, she also needed to set him straight.

Challenge him.

"I really didn't like your energy earlier. It got dark real quick."

Emmett's eye darkened, and his lips flattened into a thin line. He was quiet for a moment but then nodded before he spoke. "It did. You're right. I apologize. Liam can be a bit much sometimes. His cavalier attitude about things is a bit of a trigger for me. He's been divorced a lot longer than I have and has come to terms with his life, his relationships and love. I guess as much as I say I no longer believe in happily ever after, perhaps a small sliver of me is still holding out hope. I've never had a *relationship of convenience* before, so I just don't understand his and Richelle's deal." He ran his finger down her cheek again, his eyes boring into her, seeking approval and acceptance. "But there was no excuse for how I acted or how I treated my friend. You're right."

She smiled. "Daisy gave you a glowing reference, sang nothing but your praises."

"Did she now?"

"Mhmm. Seemed positively giddy with the notion of us getting together."

"Giddy, huh?"

"Yes, giddy."

She licked her lips, then slid her tongue along his. "I want to get to know you better. See past the dark energy from earlier, the jaded divorcee and tired single dad."

"Describes me to a T," he said, amusement in his tone, but not without a hint of irony and sadness either. "That's a lot of pressure on a guy to make sure you see more than that."

She gripped his hair tighter in her fingers, angled her head and mouth over his. "Yeah, but something tells me a doctor-astronaut-cop like you is up for the challenge." His lips meshed with hers once again, his kiss fierce and demanding, taking over, and insisting she give him more. She met his tongue and gave it teasing, lascivious laps with her own, loving the way he sucked and nibbled on her bottom lip, only to drive his tongue deep into the recesses of her mouth. Always keeping her on her toes, mixing it up and showing her just how *skilled* he was.

She could only imagine.

They made out like that for a while. Nothing but heavy petting, lots of kissing and temptation for what could be if they only had the balls to close the door.

She was about to suggest such a thing, give in to the temptation and the raging hormones inside her, when footsteps coming down the hall at a frantic pace interrupted her punch-drunk brain.

"Emmett?" Daisy's voice caused Emmett to pull away from her quicker than if she'd suddenly caught fire.

A young woman of about nineteen stood behind Daisy, terror on her face and baby Chelsea in the Ergo carrier on her chest.

"I don't want to freak you out, Emmett," Daisy said calmly, resting a hand on his arm, her eyes scanning Emmett and Zara's flushed faces, "but Josie appears to have gone missing."

EMMETT'S GAZE narrowed on Daisy. Every muscle in his body tightened up to the point of near snapping. "What do you mean *she appears to have gone missing?* Did she leave the house? Is my five-year-old daughter wandering the streets right now?" He was struggling to keep his tone level and his anger from flying out, hitting Daisy in the face and ruining everyone's evening.

There had to be a logical explanation for all of this. JoJo knew better than to leave. She was a smart, crazy-responsible child. She would never, ever leave.

Unless someone had taken her.

Spots clouded his vision, and he swayed where he stood, his eyes lasering in on the young woman behind Daisy. "Are you the babysitter?" He was so close to ripping somebody's head clean from their shoulders. Where the hell was The Rage Room when he needed it?

The young woman nodded. "I'm really sorry, Mr. Strong. She was in the corner doing beads with a couple of other girls one minute, and then I turned my back to go change Chelsea's diaper, and when I glanced at them again, Josie was gone."

"Have you *looked* for her?" Emmett ground out, his fists bunching at his sides.

The babysitter nodded.

Daisy squeezed Emmett's arm. "I'm sure there is a reasonable explanation for all of this. It's a big house. Maybe Josie is just hiding somewhere. Maybe she and the other kids started playing hide-and-seek. We don't know."

"Did you *ask* any of the other kids if they saw her leave? Those other two girls she was doing beads with?"

The babysitter nodded. "I did. They said they didn't see where she went."

A warm hand landed on his shoulder. "We'll go look for her together," Zara said softly. "I'm sure she's still in the house."

Emmett glared at Daisy. "How *well* do you know everybody here? Could she have been nabbed?"

Anger flashed behind the striking green in Daisy's eyes, but she kept her composure. "I understand you're worried, Emmett. So let's look for her first before we start throwing around such accusations, okay?"

She fixed him with a look of warning that he often saw her make with her son and sometimes even her husband. Daisy McMillan ran a tight ship and had no problem standing up to anybody, least of all Emmett.

He knew he needed to cool his temper, but fear made people do crazy things.

He made a noise in his throat and nodded, grumbling an apology to Daisy as he pushed passed her, shaking himself free of Zara's hand. He was down the hall and the stairs in no time, heading down more stairs to the basement, calling out "JoJo!" as he went.

"Josephine Eliza Strong, where are you? Come out, baby. No more hide-and-seek."

"Josie!" Zara called behind him, right on his heels. Her hand fell to his shoulder. "I'll go see if Nolan's seen her." Then she ducked into the big family room Daisy had set up as Grand Central for all the kids.

Emmett kept searching.

He opened door number three, hoping to find his daughter happily playing on the floor with Zelda the giraffe, only to once again come up with bubkes. No Josie, just a ... Fuck, was that a sex swing hanging from a metal frame in their home gym? Jesus! Riley and Daisy were kinky buggers.

And why the hell wasn't that door locked?

Normally, he wouldn't have locked a door in a home that wasn't his, but Riley was his best friend, and he knew for certain both Riley and Daisy would not want that door unlocked and stumbled into by anyone, particularly any of their guests' children. He pushed in the lock and shut the door behind him, hoping to God that JoJo hadn't already opened that door and then run off traumatized.

Emmett was all for a little spice in the bedroom, and he wasn't against a sex swing, but that shit needed to be kept under lock and key. And he most certainly hadn't expected to find out that his best friend and his wife were into such things.

He shook himself. He needed to get his head on straight and find his daughter. He'd been distracted with Zara upstairs. Meanwhile, his precious JoJo could be anywhere.

He came to the end of the dark hallway, no more doors to open.

Heavy breathing and heeled footsteps approached him,

panic in the heavy step. He knew the shadow before she came into view. Zara looked like she'd seen a ghost.

"Nolan is missing, too. None of the other kids have seen either of them."

Fuck!

He took off after Zara down the hall toward Grand Central again, meeting up with Daisy and the babysitter.

"Nolan is missing, too," Zara repeated. "Do you think they're hiding together?"

Daisy nodded absentmindedly. "Yeah, maybe." She glanced back down the hallway where Emmett and Zara had just come from. "You don't think they're in the wine cellar, do you?"

Wine cellar?

Emmett didn't know his best friend had a wine cellar.

"You have a wine cellar?" Zara asked.

Daisy nodded again, taking off back down the hallway. "Riley just put it in. You access it from his office. He's very proud of it. It's a door in the wall, but when you open it, it goes downstairs into a little bunker. Though it's normally locked. But he's been having trouble with the door sticking lately. The contractor is scheduled to come by and take a look at it next week. With all this moisture in the air during the winter, the wood apparently expands. The hinges are all weird too."

"Shit, maybe they got stuck down there," Emmett said. Thoughts of his sweet little JoJo bawling her eyes out on the cold concrete floor of the cellar, wondering if anybody would ever find her, made his chest tighten to a point of pain.

Deep breaths. Deep breaths.

He did just that. In through the nose, out through the mouth. In through the nose, out through the mouth.

It wouldn't do anybody any good to start panicking.

JoJo was fine. She just had to be.

Zara's hand landed on his shoulder as they followed Daisy down the hallway, the babysitter taking up the rear, sniffling and crying quietly as she bounced a warbling Chelsea.

"We'll find them," Zara said, squeezing his shoulder. "They haven't left. They're just hiding."

"I'm so sorry," the babysitter kept murmuring.

Daisy opened the door to Riley's office and flicked on the overhead light to reveal a manly room with lots of dark wood and leather. A big television sat over an ornate fireplace, and an enormous desk sat below a big window. A door, the same color wood as the desk, was positioned between two bookcases.

Emmett had been in Riley's office many times before, and where the door was now had once been another bookshelf loaded with Riley's diplomas. Those diplomas were now hung up on the wall in big, fancy frames, reminding Emmett's best friend just how accomplished he was.

Daisy *clickety-clacked* her heels over to the door between the bookcases and tried the latch. It moved. The door opened.

"That should be locked," she said ominously, pulling the door open.

Emmett elbowed his way forward, Zara right beside him.

"Josephine!" he called down the stairs. "Are you in here?"

"Nolan!" Zara called, her voice quavering, not nearly as sure or steady as a moment ago. Emmett could feel her worry. It mirrored his own.

Seconds later, two tiny faces appeared at the base of the stairs.

Relief swamped him like a dam breaking.

Oh, thank God.

He thundered down the stairs toward his daughter,

scooping her up in his arms and kissing her neck. "What on earth, JoJo-bean? Why did you come down here?"

She buried her face in his neck and squeezed him back tighter than he could ever remember her holding him. He felt her little body tremble in his, and warm droplets dripped down beneath his collar. He pulled her away from him to study her face.

She was crying.

He wandered over to a small oak barrel, tested its strength, and when he realized it would hold his weight, he sat down, perching his daughter in his lap. He cupped her face. "What happened, sweetie?"

Her chest shook. "Those girls started to be mean to me. Then they took Zelda from me and wouldn't give her back. Then they started playing tug of war with her and pulled her legs off."

Emmett's mouth dropped open.

He studied his daughter. She didn't have Zelda with her but was instead clutching a different stuffed animal—a different giraffe.

"I saw what they were doing and tried to stop them," Nolan cut in, now in Zara's arms. "I'm sorry that I couldn't stop them, Josie."

"So you ran off?" Emmett asked, turning back to face his daughter.

She wiped beneath her eyes and nodded. "Yeah. Nolan came after me and offered me Ziggy." She held up the other giraffe, which just like Zelda had seen *a lot* of love over the years. She turned to face Nolan, holding out the stuffed animal. "Thank you. He helped me."

Nolan grinned, then pushed out of Zara's arms so he could stand on his own again. "You can have him for a bit longer if you need him. I don't mind."

JoJo's grin made Emmett's heart damn near explode. She clutched the giraffe back to her chest. "Thank you."

"Did you guys get stuck down here?" Zara asked.

Nolan nodded. "Yeah, I tried the door but it wouldn't budge. It was weird. We called for help." He shrugged. "But then we figured eventually somebody would find us." He cocked his head and squinted his eyes at his mother, then turned his head and did the same thing to Emmett. "Have you two been kissing?"

Zara's eyes damn near popped out of her head. Emmett's too.

JoJo cupped his face, then used her finger to wipe something off his lip. "You're wearing lipstick, Daddy." She giggled.

"And it's all over your face, Mom," Nolan said, his nose wrinkling.

Zara's mouth dropped open. "Uh ... "

"Is it New Year's already?" JoJo asked. "Did we miss the countdown? Were we down here that long?"

"Everything okay down there?" Daisy called from the top of the stairs.

"Just getting the full story," Zara called back up. "We'll be up in a moment."

"Would ice cream make things better?" Daisy called back down. "We have it pre-scooped in little bowls in the chest freezer."

Both Nolan and JoJo's eyes lit up, and their heads nearly rolled off their necks from how hard they nodded.

"Can I, Dad?" JoJo asked, having seemed to recover from her ordeal with the other girls. "I'm just going to play with Nolan for the rest of the party. Those other girls aren't my friends. Friends don't treat each other like that."

Nolan reached for her hand. "I'll be your friend. I'll protect you," he said, helping her slide off Emmett's lap. "We'll get

Zelda back for you, and then my mom can stitch her legs back on if you want. She's stitched Ziggy's ears back on before. And ears and legs are pretty much the same for stuffed animals."

"Thank you," JoJo said, the two of them heading off toward the stairs. "Want to do a puzzle together after our ice cream?"

Nolan grinned at her as they made their way up the stairs, hand in hand. "Sure. Though I'm going to warn you, I'm really good at jigsaw puzzles. Did a thousand-piece puzzle this summer with my dad in like twenty days."

JoJo's mouth opened in awe. "That's a lot of pieces and not a lot of days."

Nolan's smile turned slightly smug, and he lifted a shoulder. "Yeah, but I managed. Wasn't too hard, and my dad helped ... a little bit."

Emmett fought back a laugh.

Zara snorted next to him and rolled her eyes.

The children reached the top of the stairs.

"We're all good?" Daisy called down.

"We're all good," Emmett replied, his heart rate having finally settled again, his chest no longer tight, his breathing back to normal. "Thanks, Daise. And sorry ... *babysitter.*" Shit, he really should have learned her name.

"Her name is Trista," Zara said, laughing next to him.

"Sorry, Trista!" Emmett called back up the stairs, rolling his eyes.

Zara snorted again.

Once they heard everyone in the office leave and the door *click* shut behind them, their eyes drifted toward each other. Still seated on the barrel, Emmett reached for her hand and pulled her toward him, spreading his knees and drawing her between them.

Daisy, that little matchmaker—she knew what she was

doing when she offered the kids ice cream and didn't encourage Emmett and Zara to return to the surface.

Well, why not take full advantage of the privacy?

He released her hand and wrapped his arms around her waist. Her hands floated up and rested on his shoulders. Once again her fingers found their way into his hair, though she seemed to be struggling a bit with her bandaged hand, and eventually it just rested on his shoulder while the other one continued to play with his hair.

"A bit of a scare there," she said.

He grunted. "Nothing like the fright of a lost child to get your adrenaline pumping." He blew out a breath and rolled his eyes. "I'd rather just ride a damn roller coaster, thank you very much. JoJo knows better than to do that kind of crap. Those girls really must have hurt her. She's very softhearted."

"Nolan knows better too," she said. "I'm just glad they were together. That they were still in the house."

He blew out a breath. "You and me both."

"Your daughter is adorable."

A small smile coasted across his mouth. "And your son is a wonderful young man. A real hero. You and his father are raising him right. A young man I would not threaten with a shotgun if he knocked on my door to pick JoJo up for a date ... when she's thirty-five, that is."

Zara tossed her head back and laughed, exposing the long, sexy line of her throat. A throat he desperately wanted to taste again. To rake his teeth up and hear her gasp above him, feel her grind her body against his.

Zara stepped closer to him, her breasts now right in front of his face. He resisted the urge to shove his face into her cleavage and set up camp there for the rest of the night.

"That's about one of the nicest compliments I've ever received in my life," she said softly, twirling the hair at the nape of his neck around her fingers. "I'd rather someone tell me I'm doing a great job with my son than say I have a nice ass any day. Looks fade, but our children are our legacy. Our children are a reflection of us ... our successes and our failures."

"Can I say both? That you're an amazing mom *and* that you have a nice ass?" he asked, his voice deepening and growing gravelly the more aroused he became. He wanted to shut his eyes and just give over to the pleasure of this incredible woman playing with his hair, but he resisted.

She laughed again, the warm puffs of air from her breath hitting his face. She smelled like wine and flowers—a heady combination, if ever there was one.

"Sure. Two compliments for the price of one. I won't say no."

He wanted to grab that nice ass—hell, that *great* ass and bring her closer. Let her know just how badly he wanted her.

"You always hope you're doing an okay job with your kids," she continued, "and in today's climate, you hope to *God* you're raising your sons to be respectful men. I'm glad it's not just me and my biased motherly love that thinks he's a great kid. Thank you, Emmett. I really needed to hear those words." She tugged just a touch on his hair, forcing his head to tilt upward. "My eyes are up here." Her lip crook said she didn't mind one bit that he'd been appreciating what was right in front of him.

"Yeah, but your tits are right here."

Her laughter made his cock jerk in his pants, which had grown incredibly uncomfortable in the last few moments.

"I love your laugh," he said, taking the risk and pressing his nose and cheeks against the tops of her soft breasts, nuzzling them.

She inched forward just a fraction more, and her pelvis grazed his erection. It jerked before he could tell it not to.

He glanced up at her, not removing his nose from her chest.

Her eyes flared.

"What are we doing, Emmett?" she breathed, her chest now heaving against his face, her feminine scent driving him absolutely bonkers.

His fingers bunched in the fabric of her dress, drawing it up her legs until her ass was exposed. He cupped her almost bare bottom, loving the way her cheeks clenched in his palm. He could tell she worked out, or at least walked a lot. Her thighs, although soft, had muscle and definition, the same with her ass. Each cheek was the perfect handful—and then some. He could only imagine how amazing that ass would look up in the air with her bent over the wine barrel and his cock sliding in and out of her.

She was curvy in all the right places. Something to hold on to. Feminine and beautiful.

"Emmett?" Her words were now a strangled murmur as he brought one hand around under her dress and pushed her panties to the side, exploring her slick folds.

She was so wet for him already.

"Hmm?" he hummed, tracing trails over the tops of her breasts with his tongue.

"What are we doing?"

"I don't know," he whispered, kissing the swell of each perfect mound, wishing he had more hands so he could still cup her ass, explore her pussy but also fish her breasts out of her top and draw a tight nipple into his mouth. "What I do know is that you're making me break all my rules. This isn't typical me at all."

Her breath snagged, and gooseflesh broke out across her chest and arms. He glanced up at her but didn't stop the exploration of his tongue. She was staring down at him with an open mouth and wide eyes, her cheeks gorgeously pinked up and sexy as fuck.

She closed her mouth, and her top teeth slid along her bottom lip. "Well ... we should probably figure that out before it goes any further, no? I don't have any *protection* on me. And I'm not on any kind of birth control."

"I have a condom in my pocket," he murmured, tracing his tongue down her cleavage. He released her butt cheek and palmed her breast, drawing one out from the top of her dress and finally getting to taste her sweet strawberry-red nipple.

"You have a condom?" She jerked away from him just slightly. "So you were expecting to get laid tonight?"

She hadn't pulled away enough, and his fingers were still in her panties. He flicked her clit with his thumb, and the woman spasmed right before his eyes. He had to keep himself from laughing. It was a struggle.

"So were you just looking for tail tonight, didn't really care where you got it? Would any one of those women have sufficed? That stunning redhead I saw you chatting up, was she on your radar too?"

His eyes flicked up from her one exposed breast and that deliciously tight nipple to her eyes. Fire, blue and fierce, stared back at him in challenge—in defiance.

He liked it.

Her rubbed her nub again, and the woman quivered where she stood. Her eyes fluttered, and her lips parted. A rush of wetness flowed from her core, soaking his hand.

"I *always* carry a condom on me, Zara. Always. Whether it's for a friend, for myself, or whatever. I have *always* had a condom in my pocket since college. It's the responsible thing to do. Just like I also *always* have Band-Aids in my pockets." He shifted where he sat on the barrel and reached into his pants pocket, his other hand still happily beneath her skirt, his thumb on the trigger. He pulled out the condom and a small little plastic to-go pack of Band-Aids.

Her eyes narrowed as she took the Band-Aid pack from him. "Why?"

"Because I'm a father, I'm a doctor, and I'm a responsible forty-year-old man. You'd be surprised how many times that pack of Band-Aids has come in handy. Either for JoJo or another kid at the park or wherever. I have a full first aid kit in the back of my SUV too."

"And the condom?" She placed the Band-Aids in his palm and picked up the condom. "Why do you *always* have a condom on hand?"

"Because the one time I didn't have a condom on hand, I missed the opportunity to have sex with one of the prettiest cheerleaders on the squad. She wasn't easy, she wasn't someone all the guys took a turn with, but she was somebody they all *wanted*. We were at a party one night. She took me up to a room, got naked and said she wanted me to take her virginity. I nearly came right then and there."

Zara's glare ebbed and her lip twitched, quirking up into a lopsided smile.

Good.

"Only I didn't have a condom on me. She shrugged, got dressed and left. She ended up getting a ride home from some astrophysics major. They started dating. I think they're even married now. But after that night, I vowed never, ever to be unprepared again. You never know when you're going to need a Band-Aid—"

"Or a condom," she finished, stepping back into him, her voice a deep and sexy purr.

He grinned up at her, pulled her hard against him so she knew precisely how much he wanted her. "Exactly."

7

FOR THE SECOND time that night, Zara hardly recognized herself.

Who was this wild, wanton woman, currently getting felt up by a man in a wine cellar?

The same wild, wanton woman who had made a quick exit from one handsome doctor whose hand had found her knee, to go and make out with another handsome doctor in one of the guest bedrooms in her host's home.

And *that* handsome doctor currently had his hand beneath her panties and his thumb on her clit.

Zara swallowed, her pulse thumping hard and loud in her ears as she brought her unbandaged hand down from his neck and between them, feeling the hard length of him.

What I do know is that you're making me break all my rules. This isn't typical me at all.

This man just knew all the right things to say.

She couldn't remember the last time she'd ever made a man break his rules for her—possibly ever.

She wanted to know what he meant by that. What were

these rules that he valued so much, that he was compromising to be with her?

Did he normally date intellectuals? Women with educations? Was he slumming it with a florist?

You're overthinking things again.

Too fucking bad. She had to know.

She released his cock, instead resting her hand back up on his shoulder. His intense gaze followed her movements, his brows pinching together in curiosity.

"What do you mean you're breaking all your rules?" she asked. "Am I not someone you typically ... "

Date? Sleep with? Kiss? Have sex with on an oak barrel? How could she finish that question without sounding like a complete idiot?

Was she unattractive and he was throwing her a bone?

What?

"I don't normally date ... anymore," he said quietly, flicking her clit again with his thumb. "At least I haven't since my divorce. And if I did start dating, I would wait a hell of a long time before I introduced anybody to my daughter. My ex and I have an agreement—not that she really followed it— that we would wait six months to introduce JoJo to anybody we were dating."

Oh!

Dating.

Her body betrayed her brain, and she felt another gush of warm wetness flow from her and cover his hand. The flare of his eyes said he felt it and understood far more than he was letting on. All that changed was the heat in his eyes, but that alone made her nipples pebble to excruciatingly tight points.

"And I've already met your daughter," she breathed.

"You have."

"What does that mean?"

"I don't know. All I know is that I like you and I want you."

He pushed two fingers into her channel and began to pump, his hand cupping her mound and his thumb beginning to rub back and forth over her swollen and slippery clit. "I want *this*."

Zara trembled in his arms. Her eyes slammed shut, and she struggled to stay standing, but his free arm wrapped back around her and slid beneath her dress, cupping her butt and holding her tight against him. Holding her in place.

"I want this too," she whispered, not bothering to open her eyes.

He latched back onto a nipple and sucked it hard and deep into his mouth, enough to cause a snap of pain to blossom through her chest, only to pool into a warmth deep in her belly.

His fingers continued to pump inside her, grazing the walls of her pussy—he probably had to swat away a few cobwebs in the process.

"It's been a while for me," he murmured against her nipple. "And you're the perfect woman to end that dry spell."

She laughed. "I bet I've got you beat there."

His thumb picked up speed on her clit. "So we both need this?"

Zara slid her tongue along her bottom lip, her hips jerked, and she ground down on his hand. "I *so* need this."

A deep, masculine growl rumbled through his chest, making her pussy quiver.

Before she knew what was happening, Emmett had pulled his fingers free of her, his other hand from her ass, and she found herself being picked up, spun around and her butt plunked down on the hard, wooden top of the oak barrel.

What the?

She whimpered. What was going on?

Emmett sank to his knees and pushed her legs apart, cupping her butt once again and encouraging her to scoot closer toward him. Then his warm, strong, capable hands slowly, ever so fucking painfully slowly, pushed the hem of her dress up her thighs. His touch left a trail of fire along her sensitive skin.

She gripped the edge of the barrel and leaned back, letting her face tilt skyward and her eyes close.

He had all the right moves, just the right touch to make her body give over to his completely, take what he was offering and double her own offer in return.

His fingers crept up her inner thigh, followed by the heat and dampness of his tongue. He swirled that strong muscle over the spot on her panties that directly covered her clit. She shook, her legs beginning to tremble, her arms growing weak. She wasn't going to last long if his torture remained this *en pointe*.

"So responsive." He hummed, planting a kiss on her clit, before he pulled her stretchy, lacy panties to the side and sucked hard on her tender nub. "Ah fuck, you taste good."

Oh God.

He made sure her panties were out of the way, then spread her wide with two fingers and drew his tongue up between her folds, laving at her slick, swollen clit before drawing it back down to her center. The same two fingers as before swirled around her entrance, teasing her, making her moan and groan and clench.

"Emmett," she breathed, needing more, needing all of him. She wanted to tell him to quit playing but at the same time tell him to never stop. The playing, the foreplay was just too damn good. But it also told her just how skilled he was and that more of him, all of him would be all the better.

He didn't respond but instead pushed those two fingers inside her, stroking her inner walls, rubbing that sweet spot only her vibrator tended to visit these days.

His tongue raked back up her cleft and set up camp on

her clit, alternating between hard sucks and decadent, toe-curling swirls.

"Gonna come for me, Zara?" he murmured, not ceasing his efforts as he spoke.

His words sent a blissful vibration roaring through her that made her take another dozen steps toward the top of the cliff. She was teetering now. Two toes hung over the edge, and it wouldn't take more than a strong gust of wind or a little nudge to send her flying.

"Zara?" he asked again. "Gonna come, baby?"

Hell, yes, she was going to come.

"Yes," she panted, not bothering to open her eyes. Her bandaged hand was beginning to throb as she rested all her weight on her hands, but she didn't care. The pleasure masked the pain, pushed it clear out of her consciousness.

"Good girl," he purred, before sucking hard on her clit once again. "You taste so fucking good."

Why did that turn her on so much?

Because no man has ever spoken such dirty words to you before, and you love it.

He pushed a third finger inside her, drew her clit deep into his mouth, and she detonated. The man didn't nudge her off the cliff, he full-on heaved her off, but instead of falling, she flew. She floated.

Up, up, up into the stratosphere Zara soared, every neuron in her brain firing at the same time, every cell in her body clenching and releasing, pulsing in time with her raging heartbeat.

Her body went rigid at the pinnacle of her release, starburst and bright lights flashing behind her closed eyelids. And all the while, Emmett's efforts never waned. If anything, he became even more dedicated, pressing up hard on her G-spot with one or more of his fingers.

The man was skilled.

Finally, once the spasms in her limbs ebbed and she knew where she was, who she was and who she was with, she let her eyes lazily flutter open, taking in the man still on his knees in front of her. Her chest rose and fell at an erratic rate, and her pussy pulsed from the memory of his attentions.

Emmett pulled his finger from her and sat back on his heels. He gazed up at her with the satisfaction of a man who'd just finished his favorite meal but was eager for a second helping.

Her eyes roamed his face, taking in the droplets of her arousal that coated his short beard, the sheen of her release like a gloss on his lips. He brought his fingers to his mouth and, one by one, with a gleam of almost defiance in his hooded amber eyes, he licked them clean.

Zara's mouth opened in a quiet awe, watching him savor her flavor. She thought for sure he'd close his eyes, but he did not. He kept his focus on her, challenging her, intriguing her. Arousing her.

"Whoa," she breathed when he pulled the last of his fingers from his mouth.

With the grace of a lithe jungle predator, he stood up, his need for her very present at the front of his trousers. She bet he was mighty uncomfortable.

Well, she could certainly help him with that.

Repositioning herself on the barrel so she wasn't putting all of her weight on her bum hand, she reached for him, grabbing him by the waist of his pants and tugging him forward between her legs.

He reached out and bracketed her waist, rubbing the arc of her hip bones with his thumbs.

"That was ... " She gazed up at him.

One side of his shiny lips lifted up in a cocky smirk. "Yeah?"

Her eyes grew wide, and she nodded vigorously. "Yeah!"

Now his smile was full, both sides of his mouth crooked up, the corners straining to reach his ears. Oh, he wasn't just cocky. He was downright arrogant about his success.

Oh, well, she would be too if he'd reacted the same way once she took him in her mouth.

Her eyes dipped to his belt and the button of his pants. She licked her lips, reaching for the buckle.

His hand released one hip bone and fell to hers. "We don't have to," he said, his voice a deep rumble that made her lady parts begin to tingle again, demanding an encore from his very skilled fingers and tongue.

She swatted his hand away, a lopsided smile of her own curling up on the left side of her mouth. "We don't. But I want to." She made quick work of his belt, button and zipper, fishing him out of his black boxer briefs and bringing the silky smoothness of his handsome cock into her left hand. Thank God she was a lefty and it was her right that had the bandage.

With one hand still on her hip, his other one cupped her jaw and tilted her head up. His eyes searched her face. "I don't need that right now, baby," he whispered, running the pad of his thumb over her chin, then her bottom lip. "What I need is to be inside you."

Unable to stop herself, Zara closed her eyes and leaned her face into his palm. "I want that too," she replied, beginning to stroke him. "So badly."

"Look at me." The command in his tenor made her eyelids fly open. "Watch me."

She hadn't realized it, but she was still holding on to the condom in her bandaged hand. He released her hip and cheek and took it from her. Without breaking eye contact, he tore open the condom packet and sheathed himself like a pro. "Watch me," he repeated, hooking his hands behind her knees. "Push your panties to the side."

She knew the man was a bit of a hothead, and she'd seen glimpses of the ego, but what she had no clue about was how freaking alpha he turned when he went carnal. No *please*, no *thank you*. He didn't ask. He just took. He just demanded.

And if Zara was going to be completely honest with herself, she really fucking liked it.

"Panties," he grunted, releasing one of her legs and grabbing hold of his cock, stroking it and waiting for her to do her part in their little *adult* dance.

"Right. Sorry." Her head was still spinning from the last orgasm. Not all the blood had returned to her brain. And it was about to get rerouted again.

She did as she was told, tugging her panties to one side, her fingers slipping and sliding over her slick folds, her still-swollen clit. She shivered just slightly when she knocked it with her knuckle, then again when she ran circles around it with the pad of her finger.

He grunted. "Getting impatient, Zara." His hand ran up and over his length a few more times. "Should I leave you to yourself?"

Her eyes went wide. Crap, she'd been playing with herself.

"Sorry," she breathed, removing her finger from her clit and simply holding her panties to the side.

He still hadn't pulled his eyes from her, and although his mouth was set in an almost scowl, his eyes held a twinkle of amusement that warmed her from the core outward.

"Don't close your eyes," he ordered. "I want to see every single one of your reactions. Every single thing you feel." He ran the head of his latex-encased cock up and down through her slippery folds, pushing it into her channel just an inch or so, only to pull it back out and continue with his torment.

"Please," she panted, her hands on his shoulders, the fingers of her good hand digging into his skin to hold on as shards of pleasure shot through her each and every time his crown knocked her clit. "Please."

"Please, what?"

"Fuck me," she whispered, grinding against him, digging her nails into his back.

His mouth hovered over hers. She could taste her release on his breath. His fingers behind her knees tightened their grip, and he surged forward, sheathing himself inside her all the way to the base.

She let out a contented sigh.

Emmett did too.

There was really nothing like that first thrust.

God, how she'd missed that first thrust.

It was going on four years since she'd had a good *first thrust*. Four years since she'd had sex. Four freaking years. And that last time hadn't even been very good.

Well, maybe he had been, but he certainly wasn't memorable. She'd been sort of seeing him casually for a few months, but only when Nolan was with Michael.

Either way, the last time she had sex was nothing like now. The two were incomparable. Like a crisp autumn apple fresh off the tree versus an orange that had fallen from the tree and was half rotten on the ground covered in fruit flies. Yeah, apples and oranges.

She loved apples.

"Open your eyes, Zara," Emmett's deep voice demanded.

She hadn't even realized she'd closed them. She was just too far gone into the euphoria, into the abyss to remember the rules, remember her orders.

She did as she was told, and then he began to thrust. In and out, in and out, all the way out to the tip, then *alllllll* the way back in to the hilt. And slow too. So. Fucking. Slow. Torturously slow. Decadently slow. Perfectly slow.

Oh so fucking perfectly slow.

He knew exactly what he was doing too. She was a glass house, every emotion she felt right out for the world to see, so Emmett could totally see how frustrated she was with his speed or lack thereof. And he made no attempt to hide his amusement.

"Faster ... *please*," she begged, attempting to get him to move faster by rocking her hips on the barrel. That only caused it to wobble.

Shit.

"Faster?" he asked, as if he'd never heard that word before in his life. "You mean you don't like this speed?" Oh, he was a funny one. A real *funny* guy.

"Hard and fast," she pleaded. She felt like she was going to black out. It was all too much. The sensations inside her— all incredible—were zooming around in complete disarray. It was only a matter of time before they collided and her entire world exploded.

"You're sure?" he asked, not speeding up even just a little bit. "Hard and fast is what you want?"

She moved her good hand down from his shoulder and cupped his butt as best she could, pulling him closer to her with all her might. "Yes, please. Harder, faster."

His eyelids dropped to half-mast, and his grip behind her knees intensified. "All right, if you say so." Then his cadence sped up, and he began to hammer into her. He lunged forward and covered her mouth with his, smothering her quick, sharp inhale, which was followed by a whimper as the orgasm speared through her. She rocked against him, not slowing down. The orgasm blossomed from her center outward, reaching from the tip of her curling toes to the top of her head.

She encouraged him to take her even faster, even harder. She released her grip on his ass only long enough to push his pants down enough so she could feel his skin beneath her fingertips. She dug her nails into the taut, flexing flesh of his ass and held on tightly.

He used her mouth to stifle his own groans. He stilled, and his cock inside her began to pulse as he finally found his own release.

He broke their kiss moments later and buried his face in her neck, grunting as he powered forward one last time, spilling the rest of himself inside the condom.

His rapid breath was warm against her neck before he lifted his head.

"So much for *look at me, watch me*," Zara said with a big smile, not wanting him to go soft and leave her. She liked where they were, the position they were in and him safely inside her. Why did it have to end?

His glassy eyes softened. "I got caught up in the moment." He smiled before sweeping his lips across her cheek until he found her mouth. He didn't kiss her though.

"Me too." Her heart felt light, her body pliant and satisfied. The grin on her face grew wider, and she could feel his smile against hers. She squeezed his butt cheek. He clenched it in her palm, making them both laugh, their lips touching but still not kissing.

"Happy New Year, Zara," he whispered.

"Happy New Year, Emmett." And just before he took her mouth again, she wondered what it would be like to spend every New Year's Eve with Dr. Emmett Strong, to get to kiss him when the ball dropped. Ring in the new year with a big beautiful bouquet of orgasms—yeah, she thought it sounded like a pretty great way to welcome the new year, to welcome *every* new year.

8

Her collarbone left a pool of shadow in which he buried his mouth, tracing his tongue along the delicate bones of her clavicle, then back up her neck.

There was no doubt about it, Zara Olsen was a stunning woman—an incredible woman—and Emmett found himself confused and also sad when he finally began to grow soft and was forced to leave the warm, tight safety of her body.

She whimpered when he pulled free. He felt the same way.

But he also only had one condom on him—so if they were going to do this again, it'd have to be another time, or he'd go speak to Riley about bumming some prophylactics.

If that happened, his host and best friend would have a smile noticeable from space.

He scanned the well-lit wine cellar for a sink or something to help her clean up, and lo and behold, there was not only a sink in the far corner, but a roll of paper towels and a garbage can as well. Riley thought of everything!

He made sure she was okay and not about to topple off

the wine barrel before he pulled the condom free, tied it at the top and walked over to the sink.

He tossed the condom in the trash, washed his hands and face, then folded up a paper towel, running it beneath warm water for Zara.

"You've got quite the friends," she said as he made his way back toward her. "A big mansion with a bomb shelter for a wine cellar." She whistled. "I certainly don't have friends like this."

She went to take the paper towel from him, but he shook his head and instead wiped her himself. It was the least he could do.

Her smile was shy and almost demure, but the heat in her eyes said she liked that he'd taken control once again. That he was taking care of her.

He felt better in control. Though he'd lost it a bit when he came, squeezing his eyes shut and kissing her after he'd demanded she look at him the entire time. Yeah, the control freak didn't have much control then.

He didn't like losing control. Didn't like it at all. And as much as he was trying to hold on to that post-orgasm euphoria, something began to niggle at the back of his neck. He'd lost control around this woman. She'd met his child. As much as she felt right in his arms, this was not how things were supposed to go.

"Thank you," she whispered once he was finished and walked back over to the garbage.

He returned to her and helped her off the oak barrel. He'd never be able to look at that barrel or this wine cellar the same way again.

She offered him her hand. "I'm famished. Should we go find something to eat?" Shoving down the weird feelings that stirred inside him, Emmett nodded and took her hand, the two of them making their way up the stairs.

"I'd like to go check on JoJo, if you don't mind. She seemed okay when she left, and she hates it when I hover or *helicopter parent,* as they say, but I would still like to go see how she's getting on."

She squeezed his hand. "Of course. I'm sure Nolan is taking great care of her."

They reached the top of the stairs, both of them turning inward to look back down into the cellar. He glanced sideways at Zara. She was biting her lip to keep her smile small.

His grin was huge.

"That was fun," she said, turning to face him.

"It was. Best new year's I've had in a long time."

Her bright blue eyes glittered. "Me too."

He heard her stomach rumble. "Let's feed you." Then with one final glance back into the cellar, he tugged her off the landing and back out into Riley's office, shutting *and* locking the cellar door before they retreated out into the hallway.

Voices down the hall toward kid Grand Central Station could be heard—all of them happy. Murmurs, laughter and the tinkling sound of utensils rumbled upstairs.

"Can we just stay down here the rest of the night?" Zara asked as they approached the big playroom.

Emmett abruptly released her hand and took a large step away from her, causing her expression to turn curious. "Wouldn't that be nice?" he said, hoping his smile subdued her. He spied JoJo off in the corner with Nolan, the two of them sitting on the floor surrounded by puzzle pieces. She didn't even notice him approach.

"Looks like you two are having fun," Zara said, standing awfully close to Emmett, the two of them watching their children's heads bob, though neither kid bothered to look up. Emmett took a half step away from Zara, earning another curious glance from her. He just didn't want JoJo to get the wrong idea about him and Nolan's mother. The kids had already accused them of kissing. He didn't want to confuse his daughter even more. Not like how his ex-wife had confused her when she introduced JoJo to her new boyfriend.

Apparently, the first time his ex-wife introduced JoJo to her new boyfriend Huntley, Tiff had let him sleep over, and that did not sit well with JoJo. They'd locked their bedroom door and slept in the next morning, leaving JoJo to figure out breakfast on her own.

Their daughter had also started having nightmares after the divorce and was prone to waking up at night and in need of a cuddle. JoJo said she'd had a nightmare that night, but Tiff hadn't heard her crying, and when JoJo went to go find her mom, she found the door locked and didn't know what to do after that. She didn't feel comfortable going into the bedroom with Huntley there, so JoJo had simply gone back to bed and cried herself to sleep.

Then, according to his daughter, Huntley had wandered out of the bedroom in his underwear—the short, nut-hugging, white kind—and proceeded to eat breakfast in his underwear too. His daughter had been mortified.

Emmett and Tiff wound up having quite the fight about all of it when JoJo came to him the following day and told him everything. She didn't want to go back to her mother's if Huntley was going to be there. She didn't like how he'd made himself at home in her home and that she couldn't go to her mother when she needed her at night.

Emmett couldn't blame his daughter, but Tiff said they were both overreacting.

Things became quite heated.

And even though JoJo didn't seem to have any issues with Zara, he still didn't really like that he hadn't been able to control how his daughter met the woman he was interested in. It all made him very nervous.

Lack of control in general made him nervous.

"Josie is helping me do this puzzle," Nolan said, still not bothering to look up at Emmett or Zara.

"We're helping each other," JoJo corrected, tucking a strand of her long blonde hair behind her ear.

Nolan nodded absentmindedly, his cheeks turning slightly ruddy. "Right. Right. Sorry."

"Well, it's so nice to see you two playing together," Zara said. "And Josie, I'd be more than happy to fix your giraffe. I could probably have her back to you by tomorrow."

JoJo finally lifted her head. She squinted at Emmett, then her eyes shifted over to Zara. Emmett felt his unease spike, and he instantly took another half step away from Zara, causing her brows to furrow and her nostrils to flare. She glanced sideways at him, then her jaw flexed.

"Thanks," JoJo finally said, before she put her head back down and resumed searching for puzzle pieces.

"Perhaps we could all grab breakfast in the morning," Zara said, hope in her voice, which immediately made the hair on the back of Emmett's neck stand up. He was already going against all his rules, letting a woman he was interested in meet his daughter—though he really had no choice in the matter—but he had to draw the line somewhere about JoJo spending any time with a new person who Emmett was romantically interested in. A loving mother or not.

Zara was trying to assume control, and he didn't like it.

He had rules. He and Tiff had an agreement.

Yeah, but it's not like she stuck to her end of that agreement.

Yeah, but two hypocrites didn't cancel each other out, and he didn't want to confuse his daughter or give her false hope. He also didn't want her getting too attached to Nolan—or Zara, in case things between him and Zara went south.

There was just so much to consider before he started to let his daughter spend time with Zara—or any woman he was dating. He couldn't just flippantly make that decision without weighing all the pros and cons, without getting to know Zara on his own. What if their chemistry was falsified by the whimsy of the night and they really had absolutely nothing in common? What if, when the sun came up tomorrow, they were like opposing magnets, rather than unable to keep their hands off each other? What then? How could he explain that to his daughter?

Yes, he liked the woman standing next to him, found her to be exquisite in every which way—at least the ways he'd gotten a chance to know in the last twelve hours—but their relationship or whatever it was was still really new.

Had JoJo or Nolan not been at the party already, he never would have introduced his daughter to Zara, and he would have expressed concern and reluctance if Zara insisted Emmett meet Nolan so quickly as well.

No matter how much he liked Zara, his daughter was his world, and he would not disrupt her happiness for anything. He would not confuse her or put her under any undue stress or upset, not if he could help it. She'd already been through so much when he and Tiff divorced, he wouldn't do that to her again. Not for anybody.

He had rules for a reason. He'd resisted dating this long for a reason.

"Can we, Dad?" JoJo asked, interrupting his thoughts. He glanced back down at his daughter. Now both she and Nolan were staring at him with puzzled expressions and impatient eyes.

"Can we what?" he asked.

"Go for breakfast tomorrow, all of us. Nolan and I are becoming good friends."

Emmett swallowed. "We'll see, honey. You might be really tired tomorrow."

His daughter's nose wrinkled, and one shoulder

shrugged. "Then we go for lunch. Or dinner."

"I like The Lavender and Lilac Bistro," Nolan said. "Have you been?"

JoJo's eyes went wide, and she nodded vigorously. "I *love* that place. We know the owner, and she always adds an extra cookie into the bag for me."

"I need to know the owner too," Nolan said, his own eyes going wide. "I love their white chocolate pound cake cupcakes. I wonder if I met the owner if she'd throw *two* cupcakes into the box for me?"

JoJo shrugged again. "Maybe. I do not know." She glanced back up at Emmett. "So lunch, Dad? Can we?"

Both JoJo and Nolan were staring at him with hopeful eyes. He slid his own eyes sideways to Zara. She had remained awfully quiet throughout. But it was her mention of breakfast that had gotten the kids on the bandwagon. And once kids jumped on, the wagon tended to gain speed and run off the road, often crashing into a tree and bursting into flames.

Emmett cleared his throat. "We'll have to see, JoJo. I need to get in touch with your mother about her plans for tomorrow. I wasn't supposed to have you tonight, remember? Your mom might want you back in the morning."

His daughter made a noise in her throat and then rolled her eyes. "She and Huntley will just sleep in after their party." She crossed her arms over her chest and sat back dramatically in a petulant little huff. "You never let me do anything fun."

Emmett's brows lifted on his forehead. "Keep up the attitude and my *maybe* will turn into a hard *no* pretty darn quick, young lady." He kept his tone kind but firm. He knew his daughter was tired. All the kids probably were. Normally, JoJo was in bed by seven thirty, eight at the latest. Perhaps he should go find Daisy and see if he could put JoJo to bed in a guest room upstairs. Or maybe he should just take his daughter home. He hadn't had much to drink. He was okay to drive.

His daughter's brows pinched; her lips jutted out into an enormous pout, and she stared down her little nose at Emmett's shoes. "I won't be tired. Can you text Mom and tell her I'm going for breakfast with Nolan and his mommy?" Oh, she was tired all right. The whine that accompanied her plea was one of her biggest tells. Normally a very agreeable child, JoJo turned quite whiny and almost confrontational when she was sleep-deprived.

He crouched down and opened his arms wide. "I think somebody is tired and needs a Daddy hug before she says something that could land her in trouble. I don't like the road we're on here, Josephine."

Slowly, JoJo lifted her gaze. Her eyes were so red. Her mouth now turned down, trembling as she fought back the tears.

His heart ached for her.

His poor little JoJo. So strong. So tired.

She fell forward onto her hands and knees and crawled toward him, launching herself into his arms. A muffled little cry seeped out from where she'd tucked her face into his neck. "I'm sorry, Daddy," she whispered.

He hugged her back tightly, running his hands down her small back, feeling her shake softly in his arms. "It's okay, sweetie. Should we get going?"

He heard a sharp inhale above him and lifted his gaze to Zara. She was now letting her gaze circle the room, though he couldn't mistake the dash of crimson that had flooded her cheeks.

"No, Daddy," JoJo whined. "I want to stay."

"Okay, but what about taking a little rest? We could go find Aunt Daisy and see if you could go curl up on one of the guest beds for a little while." He turned his wrist over and glanced at his watch. It was ten thirty. His child was not going to make it to midnight.

JoJo nodded against his neck before lifting her head, her eyes damp from fresh tears. "Okay, but will you come wake me up for the countdown?"

"I will." He brushed the hair off her forehead and out of her eyes, tucking it behind her ears. She'd just gotten her ears pierced a month ago and was still wearing the little yellow gold heart studs with tiny diamonds in the center. She was so proud of herself for getting them—told anyone who would listen that she "didn't even cry a little bit."

"Promise?" She sniffled, wiping the back of her wrist beneath her nose before holding her hand up with her pinky out. "Pinky swear?"

He linked his pinky with hers. "I swear."

With a groan, he stood up with his daughter still in his arms. Zara had retreated a few steps back to give Emmett and JoJo some space, and she was talking quietly with Nolan. Both their heads lifted when Emmett approached them. "I'm going to take JoJo upstairs and see if we can find her a quiet room to rest in for a bit."

Zara reached out and rested her hand on JoJo's shoulders, her eyes kind and motherly. "That sounds like a good idea, sweetheart. I know NoNo here is pretty tired too." She wrapped her hand around her son's shoulders and tugged him against her.

Nolan glared up at her. "Mom," he gritted, "I don't like that nickname anymore. I'm a big kid. I called myself that when I was a baby. I'm not a baby anymore."

Zara's lip twitched. "Right. I forgot. Sorry, sweetheart."

Nolan's expression of irritation relaxed, and he exhaled, his shoulders slumping in fatigue. "It's fine."

Zara rolled her eyes at Emmett and smiled.

Something akin to agitation niggled and tickled the back of Emmett's neck, seeing Zara's hand on his daughter's shoulder. His eyes flicked back and forth from JoJo's shoulder to Zara's face until the woman removed her hand, hurt and caution flaring in her blue eyes. Her mouth dipped into a sad frown.

"I'm not tired," Nolan said, the same whine as JoJo's making Emmett cringe.

"That tone tells me you are," Zara said. "I think maybe we'll head home."

Fuck, Emmett was confused. He didn't want her to leave.

That was the last fucking thing he wanted.

"I don't want to head home," Nolan whined again. "I want to stay with Josie. I want to see the countdown. I want to see the ball drop."

"We could go to the bunk beds," JoJo suggested, her little mouth opening into an enormous yawn. She knuckled her eyes with one hand, holding on around Emmett's neck with the other.

Nolan nodded. "I could have a short nap, maybe."

"First we need to clean up the puzzle," Zara said, wandering past Emmett and JoJo, deliberately avoiding his gaze.

They hadn't spoken *to* each other since they entered the room. Was she just taking her cues from him that he wanted to keep their dalliance on the DL, or was she upset with him?

"I'll help too," JoJo said, leaping out of Emmett's arms and skipping the few feet toward the puzzle, where Zara and Nolan now knelt on the floor, picking up the pieces.

Emmett joined them, making sure he knelt down beside his daughter and *not* Zara. A move that did not go unnoticed —at least not by Zara.

They all picked up the puzzle pieces in silence, heads down. He reached for one of the last pieces at the same time

Zara did, and his hand landed on hers. He lifted his head, she lifted hers, and their eyes locked. What shone back behind the intense blue was a hurt that gutted him. Fuck, he was handling all of this *so* wrong. The last thing he wanted to do was hurt her.

She pulled her hand away as if he'd suddenly told her he had leprosy and averted her eyes. She cleared her throat and reached for the puzzle box, waiting for Nolan and JoJo to put the last pieces in before she closed it.

He needed to talk to her. He needed to explain his behavior and the sudden one-eighty he'd done. It wasn't that he wasn't interested in her. It was that everything was happening so fast—too fast. Their relationship—or whatever it was—was happening all out of order. He had zero control and he was beginning to spin out.

Nolan and JoJo stood up. Zara stood up and took the puzzle box back over to the shelf.

JoJo offered Emmett her hand. "I'll help you up, Daddy," she said, grunting as she heaved on him. Nolan joined in, grabbing his other arm, the two of them giggling as they tried with all their might to get him up off the floor. With a grin and a grunt of his own—because he was no spring chicken anymore—he helped the kids in their efforts and stood up.

"You're heavy," Nolan said, a tad out of breath.

"My dad weighs like five hundred pounds," JoJo said, her face very serious. "He's also really old."

"My mom's old too," Nolan replied, his face also very serious. "But she doesn't weigh five hundred pounds. More like two hundred or so."

Emmett rolled his eyes and chuckled through his nose. He could see out of the corner of his eye that Zara was struggling to keep a straight face.

"Let's go upstairs," JoJo said with another yawn. "I could use a break."

Nolan nodded, the two of them taking off ahead of Zara and Emmett, no longer appearing tired in the least.

The *clomp clomp* of heavy-footed children on the stairs echoed toward them. Emmett's eyes slid to Zara, and he went to open his mouth and say something, anything, when the sound of a hard fall, another fall, a *clunk* and then a wail— not JoJo's—filled the air.

Zara drew in a sharp breath. "Nolan!" She took off toward the stairs, Emmett hot on her heels.

They reached the landing and looked up the stairs. JoJo stood over a crying Nolan. "He slipped, fell and bonked his head on the banister," JoJo said. She rested her hand on his shoulder and bent at the waist. "You okay?" she asked.

Nolan was clearly not okay. The little boy continued to whimper and cry, his hand on his head as he rocked back and forth on the stairs.

Zara took the few steps two at a time until she reached him, crouching down and gently prying his hand away from his head.

Her gasp told Emmett it wasn't good.

"He's bleeding ... a lot," she said, turning back to face Emmett. "I need to get him to the ER."

Emmett ascended the few steps, stopping just below where Zara and the children were. "The ER will be slammed tonight. You're in a house with at least ten doctors. Let's get him to the bathroom, and I'll take a look."

Tears brimmed Zara's eyes, but she nodded, her throat bobbing on a hard swallow. Emmett pushed forward, asking his daughter to move. Then he scooped up Nolan and carried him the rest of the way up the stairs to the living room. A gaggle of people stood at the top of the stairs waiting to see where all the commotion was coming from. Both Riley's and Daisy's faces held equal looks of concern.

"He okay?" Riley asked, taking in the bleeding cut on

Nolan's head. "Need a hand?"

Emmett grunted and nodded. "Grab your first aid kit and meet me in the master bathroom."

Riley's head bobbed, then he took off.

"Those steps can be treacherous," Daisy said, rubbing Nolan's back. The little boy sniffled and whimpered in Emmett's arms. He was too close for Emmett to get a good look at the cut on his head, but out of the corner of his eye he saw red, and head wounds bled *a lot.*

Emmett jerked his head in the direction of Riley and Daisy's room. He'd use their enormous en suite so as to have a bit more privacy from the crowd. It also had the most amount of light in case he did need to stitch up Nolan's head. Zara zipped ahead and opened the door, then flicked on the light.

"Am I gonna need a cast?" Nolan asked, his sniffles now less frequent.

"We don't usually cast heads, buddy," Emmett said, making his way over to the long vanity and plunking Nolan's butt down on the counter. He leaned over and turned on the big round vanity lights that ran down either side of the enormous mirror.

Nolan's eyes grew saucer-size. "Stitches!"

Emmett made sure not to let his face be too expressive. He allowed his lips to flatten, then placed his hands beneath Nolan's chin to tilt the little boy's head up. "Let's not start counting chickens or anything like that. Let's just wipe up the mess and see how big the cut is. Could be a superficial scratch and you won't need more than a Band-Aid."

Nolan's lip began to tremble.

Emmett felt himself get shoved out of the way, only to find JoJo at his side. "Here," she said, thrusting Ziggy the giraffe into Nolan's arms, then she took his hand. "Now I'm here when *you're* sad."

Damn, his daughter was a sweetheart.

Nolan whimpered a little bit but hugged the giraffe tight to his chest with one hand while holding on to JoJo's hand with the other. Emmett could feel Zara behind him, feel her worry and her need to help her child in some way. He was the exact same way whenever JoJo got hurt. Even though a lot of parents were of the *let them bleed* and *walk it off* mentality, Emmett just couldn't do that. When his child was hurt, he had to help her.

Maybe it was the doctor in him and that darn Hippocratic oath he'd taken, but when someone was in pain, be it his child or someone else's, he could never just wait for them to *walk it off*.

"Here's the first aid kit," Riley said, rushing into the big bathroom and setting a bright red canvas tote down on the counter next to Emmett. He unzipped it. "Need me to scrub in with you?"

Emmett rolled his eyes at his friend. "I think I've got it. If he needs an appendectomy, we'll call you."

"What's an *app-en-dectomy?*" Nolan asked, his eyes continuing to grow wider. "That sounds serious."

Emmett grabbed a pair of latex gloves from the kit and snapped them onto his hands before he pulled a bit of gauze out of its sanitary bag. He ran the gauze under the faucet just a touch, then brought it up in front of Nolan's eyes. "I'm going to clean the cut now, okay?"

Nolan nodded. "Okay."

Emmett went to task, doing his best to be gentle, slow and explain everything he was doing before he did it.

He actually preferred child patients in the ER to adult ones. Children, although scared, were easier to distract, and they didn't feel like his explanations were patronizing to them, as some adults did. Plus, kids were just more fun in general—as long as they weren't whiny.

"Do I need stitches?" Nolan asked, his blue eyes following Emmett's every move.

Emmett twisted his lips and jostled them back and forth on his face for a moment. He'd managed to stanch the bleeding pretty well, but the cut in Nolan's hairline was rather deep.

"Maybe two," he finally said. "Otherwise, you'll wind up with a little white scar."

Nolan shrugged, though the fear in his eyes betrayed how he really felt. "Scars are cool."

"Nolan," Zara said quietly behind him, "maybe you should just listen to Emmett. He's a doctor. He knows what's best." Maybe he was reading too much into it, or perhaps it was because he couldn't see her face, but Zara's tone and the way she said his name and profession made his whole body go ice cold. She said it without an ounce of warmth, and if he wasn't mistaken, there was a bit of a bite to it as well.

"But scars are cool, Mom," Nolan persisted.

Emmett craned his neck around to look at Zara. What met him were shuttered eyes and a blank expression. He swallowed. "There is numbing gel in here, so I can do the stitches and he won't feel a thing."

Her eyebrows lifted just a fraction on her forehead, but nothing else moved. "Up to him," she said.

"No stitches," Nolan began to chant. "No stitches. Scars are cool. No stitches. Scars are cool."

JoJo joined in, both of them smiling and giggling as they pounded their fists on their laps and continued to chant.

Emmett's mouth lifted into a half smile, and he shook his head. "All right then. Let's just put a butterfly bandage on it instead." He reached into the first aid kit and grabbed a couple of the smallest butterfly bandages he could find.

"Do you have any dragon bandages?" Nolan asked. "But-terflies are *okay*, but dragons or even dragon*flies* are better."

Emmett paused, tapped his chin with his index finger, then peered back into the first aid kit. "You know, I think Riley may have one or two dragonfly bandages left. They usually get used up *first,* which is why we're only left with butterfly bandages. But let me take a look and see." He hemmed and hawed as he dug around in the bandage box, pretending to look for something that obviously wasn't there —because it didn't exist. After about twelve seconds, his brows shot up and he pulled out a regular old butterfly bandage. "Eureka! Found the last dragonfly bandage in the box."

Nolan's smile was electric. "Cool. What's the difference between a butterfly bandage and a dragonfly bandage?"

Ah, shit. Emmett should have expected a question like this. If Nolan hadn't asked it, JoJo probably would have. He peeled back the paper and placed his left hand on Nolan's forehead, pushing his hair out of the way. "Well, a butterfly bandage is just a little bit bigger and wider, because butterfly wings are bigger and wider than dragonfly wings. But the dragonfly bandage is just cooler." He finished placing the bandage over Nolan's cut. It was small enough that one *dragonfly* bandage would suffice.

Nolan nodded. "Dragonflies are cooler."

He placed a regular Band-Aid over the butterfly bandage to make sure it caught any residual bleeding, then Emmett snapped off his gloves and tossed them into the trash bin next to the toilet. He helped Nolan jump down off the vanity. "Now, take it easy. From the looks of things, you don't have a concussion. I checked your pupils while I was cleaning your cut. But if you run or jump or roughhouse, you could cause it to start bleeding again because you never let me stitch it up."

Nolan's shoulder lifted in a way that seemed far too old and far too cool for a seven-year-old. "Scars are cool, man. I'll take it easy. I promise."

"Yeah, Dad," JoJo chimed in. "He'll take it easy."

"Yes, you will," Zara cut in, stepping forward and resting her hand on Nolan's shoulder. "Because we're going to get going."

JoJo's mouth dropped open, followed by Nolan's and then finally Emmett's.

"What?" Nolan exclaimed. "We can't. What about the countdown?"

"We can do the countdown at home. You just had a big fall. You're tired. *I'm* tired."

Why did she say she was tired in such a weird way?

She also hadn't looked at Emmett once since she said they were leaving.

"But I was having fun." Nolan crossed his arms over his chest and stomped. "We were going to go sleep on the bunk beds so we could be awake for the countdown."

Zara ran her hand over her son's head, still unwilling to look at Emmett. "I know, sweetie, but it's just better if we go." Finally, she lifted her eyes to Emmett's. "Thank you for taking care of him. We're going to head home now. I can't get a read on the temperature of the *guests* here anymore. I'm tired of the hot and cold." Then she averted her gaze once again and glanced down at Nolan and JoJo. "I think you might have to ask your own mommy to stitch up your giraffe for you, honey," Zara said in a wooden tone. "Might be best."

JoJo's mouth dipped into an even bigger frown. "My mommy doesn't sew."

"I'll sew it for you, JoJo-bean," Emmett said quietly, knowing he'd screwed the pooch with Zara but unsure how to rectify it now that the kids were with them.

His daughter lifted her tired eyes to his, skepticism radiating off of her small frame in gigantic waves. "Do you even know how to sew?"

He fluffed her hair and rolled his eyes. "I stitch people up for a living, sweetie. I think I can manage."

"People and stuffed animals are *very* different."

Right! Stuffed animals were not sentient beings whom he could potentially kill, maim or scar for life. So much harder.

He fluffed her hair again. "I'll be careful."

Zara made a noise in her throat. "We should get going, honey."

Nolan grumbled, turning his body and gaze to JoJo. "Maybe we can have a playdate soon?"

JoJo nodded and said "yes" at the same time Zara said, "I don't think that's such a good idea."

Both kids' heads shot up to Zara's face.

"What? Why?" Nolan asked, that whine back in his voice.

Zara exhaled, her shoulders slumping, her eyes tired and sad. "We'll talk about it in the car, honey. Let's get going."

Nolan pouted, clutched his giraffe tighter to his chest but nodded.

Zara turned to go. Her son trudged after her, scuffing his feet.

"Can I go say goodbye to them at the door?" JoJo asked, tugging on Emmett's hand.

He nodded, not bothering to look down at his child. His eyes were glued to the back of Zara's head, willing her to turn around, for them to find an empty room or a secluded corner where they could talk. Where he could explain.

She paused on the threshold of the bathroom and Riley and Daisy's room.

Was she going to turn around? Did she realize that her leaving without them talking first was a big mistake?

She glanced behind her, her eyes deliberately fixed *not* on his face. "It was nice meeting you, Emmett." Then she walked away.

9

EMMETT TUCKED JoJo into bed on the bottom bunk in Daisy and Riley's guest room. Daisy's nieces and nephew in Canada visited often with Daisy's brother Sam and his wife, Harper, so Daisy said it just made sense to put a bunk bed in for the kids.

"Why did Nolan have to leave?" JoJo asked, yawning for the umpteenth time since Emmett had walked her down the hallway toward the bedroom, having waited in the bathroom until he knew Zara and Nolan had left.

He was such a fucking coward.

Emmett brushed hair off JoJo's face and leaned down to kiss her on the nose. "His mommy was worried about his fall and figured he'd be more comfy back in his own bed."

His daughter's mouth curled down into a frown. "Are you and his mommy fighting?"

Emmett reared back, gazing down his nose at his very astute, far too mature for her own good daughter. "What makes you say that?"

She yawned again, her eyelids heavy. "You guys didn't

smile at each other. You and mommy were the same way before she moved out."

Ah, shit.

He cupped his daughter's cheek, leaned in and gave a kiss on the forehead this time. "We're not fighting, sweetheart. I think we're all just really tired."

When he pulled away, his daughter was glaring at him. She didn't buy it for a second.

"I like Nolan. I like his mommy. I want to have a playdate with him. He was my friend when those other girls were not." She clutched a newly sewed up Zelda to her chest. Emmett had borrowed a sewing kit from Daisy and did a quick double replantation surgery on the amputated quadruped. "He gave me his—" Suddenly she bolted upright in bed, her eyes going wide. "He forgot Ziggy!" She tossed back the covers and shoved Emmett out of the way. She tossed open the bedroom door and hightailed it down the hallway. Emmett began to follow her but barely made it halfway down the hall before his huffing and puffing daughter came running back down toward him. She must have gone downstairs.

In her hands was not only Zelda, her giraffe, but Ziggy, Nolan's giraffe.

"He forgot Ziggy," she repeated, holding the well-loved giraffe up in the air.

Emmett lifted his eyebrows. "Ah, so he did. We'll have to let Aunt Daisy know so she can get Nolan back his stuffed animal."

JoJo shook her head, fighting off her hundredth yawn for the night. "No. He told me he can't sleep without him. You need to take him his stuffed animal, Daddy. Please!"

She was so tired. Her red eyes, her slouched shoulders. It was all his little girl could do to hold herself upright.

Emmett wrapped an arm around her shoulder and led her back in the direction of the guest room. "We'll figure it out, JoJo-bean. You just close your eyes." He pulled back the covers for her once again, and she climbed in, her head hitting the pillow and her eyes shutting instantly.

"Don't be mad at Nolan or his mommy," JoJo said sleepily, not bothering to open her eyes. She yawned again. "Happy New Year, Daddy."

He leaned forward and kissed her on the temple, once again tucking her long, blonde hair behind her ear. "Happy New Year, Josephine."

ZARA'S THROAT hurt from how hard she was trying to hold back the tears. She pulled back Nolan's covers and encouraged him to climb in between his outer-space-themed bedsheets.

"You look sad, Mommy," Nolan said, sitting up and cupping Zara's cheek. "You okay?"

She couldn't stop them any longer and one, then two hot tears burst free and sprinted down her cheeks. She hiccuped a small sob and leaned into her son's small, warm hand, covering it with her own hand. "I'm fine, honey. Just tired."

Tired of being treated like an unfit mother. First Marcello—he didn't even want to have children with me—and now Emmett. He wanted me to stay as far away from his daughter as possible.

His blue eyes held an understanding she dare not explore. Did her own son question her abilities as a mother? It certainly seemed to be a growing consensus among men she slept with. Perhaps they were picking up on something she wasn't.

But then Michael had a baby with you, and he's a very good judge of character. He hated Marcello nearly the moment he met the man.

And yet she'd still married him. She should have listened

to her best friend. Michael was rarely ever wrong—something he loved to remind her of too.

"Mom?" Nolan whispered, reaching over onto his nightstand to grab a tissue from the box. "Why are you sad?" He handed her the tissue.

She thanked him and blotted her eyes. "I'm just tired, sweetheart. It's been a long, busy day. I just need to close my eyes. Tomorrow, the new day and new year will be better."

He squinted at her, still not entirely convinced. But her warning look must have been enough, and she could see him abandon his need to press her for more information. Instead, his little mouth flattened into a thin line before he spoke. "I forgot Ziggy," he said calmly, not an ounce of panic coloring his tone. She'd never seen him so unaffected by not having his best friend with him when he went to bed.

Her eyes narrowed before she slowly asked, "In the car?" She knew the answer before he gave it to her.

He shook his head calmly. "No, at the party house. Can you call and have Josie's dad bring it over? Maybe set up a playdate while he's here."

Nolan couldn't have.

Could he?

Had her son orchestrated a plot to get Zara and Emmett back in the same room? Had he deliberately left behind his most beloved toy, his best friend in the entire world, so that he could see Josie again, so that Zara would have to see Emmett again?

Nolan yawned, released Zara's cheek and flopped down onto his pillow. "I'll be okay tonight without Ziggy. But not tomorrow night. We need to have breakfast or lunch with Josie and her dad so I can get Ziggy back. One night, I'll be okay. Two nights, I won't be."

He had planned the whole damn thing!

Was Josie in on it too?

Zara's head hurt. Her heart hurt.

"Will you lay with me until I fall asleep, Mama?" Nolan asked, his eyelids growing heavy.

She nodded, and he scooted over in his bed toward the wall. His bed was just a single—they wouldn't be able to manage the two of them on there for much longer.

She turned to face him. He blinked lazily and smiled.

Gently, she ran her fingers over his butterfly—oh, sorry, *dragonfly*—bandage. Thankfully it hadn't started to bleed again.

"I'm okay, Mama," he said, yawning. "It doesn't hurt anymore. Josie's dad did a great job."

Zara's heart constricted in her chest. She smiled thinly. "He certainly did."

Nolan's eyes blinked a few more times, then he didn't bother opening them again. Seconds later, his breathing became even and his lips parted just a touch—he was out.

Zara spun in the cramped bed until she was on her back, staring up at the ceiling decorated with over a hundred glow-in-the-dark stars and planets. The entire evening began to play over in her mind.

She'd never been so wrong about a person before in her life. Never.

She thought Emmett was one of the good ones.

Ah, but you never did ask him your three questions. Bouquet needed or not, the way a person answers those questions tells you everything you need to know about them.

She didn't need to know Emmett's answers to those questions to know that the man needed counseling though. Hell, they could probably see that from the space station.

The man had been like a goddamn light switch. Affectionate and practically carnal one minute, taking her in the wine cellar, making her feel like the most beautiful, desirable, incredible woman to walk the Earth, and then the next minute, he couldn't even look at her.

She was good enough to fuck in a basement but not good enough to stand next to. Not good enough to speak to his daughter, to comfort his child. In Emmett Strong's eyes, she just clearly wasn't good enough. An unfit mother and unfit partner.

What the actual fuck?

And what made him so goddamn perfect? So goddamn special?

The man was so fucking wishy-washy. So hot and cold, she was sweating and shivering around him at the same freaking time.

She understood his desire to shelter Josie, protect her from potential heartbreak and confusion, but the man took it to the extreme. Did he not allow any woman at the park or gymnastics or swimming or whatever to speak to his daughter out of fear he might or might not end up dating that woman? God forbid his child meet them before the six-month or whatever mark.

Was he that inflexible?

Was he that much of a control freak?

Did he make his life that rigid? That structured?

She couldn't be with a man like that.

Maybe it was a good thing he'd given her the cold shoulder. He saved her from what could have been months of not knowing where she stood with him while constantly trying to live up to his unrealistic expectations and inevitably always falling short.

And if she'd met him under alternative circumstances with no Josie around, how long would he have waited to introduce her to his daughter? If they passed the six-month mark and he never made any move to introduce her to his daughter, would that mean he didn't deem her worthy? That he considered her an unfit mother and their future was bleak because she'd never be around his child? Would she end up spending months, possibly years trying to live up to some hidden expectation he had in order for them to take the next step?

She was overthinking things ...

And yet ... was she?

The man had two very different sides to him. Almost like Dr. Jekyll and Mr. Hyde, only in this case, it was Dr. *Jerk-yll* and Dr. Strong, the sexy, hilarious man she'd met in the coffee shop earlier that morning.

Had it really only been just that morning?

It felt like so long ago that they'd met. Not years, obviously, but not less than twenty-four hours either.

They'd already been through so much together.

Perhaps she should dig into who his ex-wife was—he mentioned she was a dermatologist—and pay the woman a visit. Get a mole checked. See if Emmett was the crazy person in the divorce or not. Maybe she'd left him for good reason?

She grabbed her phone off Nolan's nightstand and checked the time. It was eleven forty-five.

People up and down the Pacific coast would be getting ready to ring in the new year. Getting ready to hug their loved ones, kiss their paramours or the stranger beside them and hoot and holler until the cows came home.

Not Zara though.

Would she hear the celebration at Daisy and Riley's house from her house? There were certainly enough people there, and she only lived a couple of blocks away.

Emmett had probably already forgotten about her and was snuggled up with that gorgeous redhead from earlier, his arm around her, whispering all the right things in her ear while Josie slept in the guest bedroom down the hall, none the wiser to her father's new midnight kiss companion.

She squeezed her eyes shut but then opened them again when all she saw on the backs of her eyelids was Emmett kissing that redhead.

The man had burrowed his way so deeply under her skin, he was like freaking ringworm or something.

She scratched her arm.

Now she was itchy.

Rolling her eyes, she grumbled, grabbed her phone and slid off Nolan's bed, heading toward the kitchen to go and pour herself a glass of wine.

Once she'd nearly filled the glass, she wandered into the living room. She didn't bother to flick on any lights but instead sat down in the hand-me-down recliner from her mother and turned on the television, preferring the darkness and harsh glare of the television. It better reflected her mood.

She found the television channel that had pre-recorded the ball dropping in Times Square from earlier that night and turned up the volume, sitting back into the chair and taking a *big* sip of her wine.

Seven minutes until a new year.

And once again, she would be ringing it in alone.

10

EMMETT MADE his way through the house, Ziggy in his hand. Everyone at the party seemed to have congregated in the sunken living room or dining room.

It looked like Daisy had succeeded again, at least for the night. There wasn't a person standing alone, except for Emmett.

He spied Mason standing off to the side. Well, at least he figured it was Mason. All he could really see were the backs of about five women and what he knew was biological clocks going off and ovaries exploding.

He elbowed and maneuvered his way through the crowd. Everybody was staring intently at the television, which was tuned in to Times Square. Everybody but those five women, that is.

Mason caught his eye over the heads of the slew of admirers who were not only ogling Mason and his tattoos but the sleeping baby he wore on his chest in the Ergo.

The man always had his baby in the carrier. And he always attracted a shit-ton of female attention when he did it.

Emmett often wondered if Mason did it on purpose, that he used his adorable baby as a chick magnet.

"Hey," Mason greeted him, encouraging a couple of the women to make room for Emmett. A few of them allowed their eyes to roam up and down Emmett's body.

Emmett sidled up next to his friend. "Hey." He leaned in to check on Willow, who was out like a light. "How's she feeling? You said she had the sniffles over Christmas?"

He nodded. "I think it was actually teething. Just came out as a runny nose and crankiness. But I keep checking her mouth and so far, nothing."

Emmett nodded. "They tend to do that for a while. JoJo didn't start getting teeth until about eight months old, yet I swear she started *teething* at like two months."

Mason grumbled. "Lovely. So I have at least another four months of these restless nights until anything actually pops out?" He stroked his finger over his daughter's chubby little flushed cheek, which made the women around them croon.

Emmett shrugged. "She might pop teeth sooner. All babies are different."

"Liam and Scott said you were getting to know Zara Olsen." Mason craned his thick neck around, using his height to his advantage and glancing out over the heads of the crowd. "I don't see her."

Unease began to slither its way up Emmett's spine. How did the built, dark-haired, tattooed corporate executive-turned-bar-owner know Zara? Had they dated?

Mason's mouth slid into a sly grin, and he reached out and slapped a hand on Emmett's shoulder, squeezing it. "Relax, bro. Zara's my florist. I won't go anywhere else to get my mama a bouquet for Mother's Day, her birthday, or just because."

More feminine moans and coos echoed around them.

"I love a man who treats his mother well," one woman said. "Says so much about what kind of a husband he'll be."

Emmett's eyes flared, and he lifted his eyebrows, careful to make sure Mason was the only person who saw his reaction.

Mason simply smiled a big grin that Emmett was sure caused a few more hearts to flutter. "Zara's a real sweetheart. She'd be good for you. Where is she?"

Emmett swallowed. "She went home."

"Why?"

"Because I can't get my head on right, and I think I fucked it all up."

Mason's brows pinched, and he opened his mouth to say something, but Daisy and Riley were back up in front of the hearth, and Daisy was tapping a spoon to her champagne flute.

"All right, everyone. We're less than a minute to midnight!"

Murmurs and shuffles resonated around the room as people got into position.

Emmett spied Scott off in the corner with the brunette from earlier. Scott lifted his champagne flute in Emmett's direction and grinned that infamous Dixon smile, all while squeezing the brunette closer to him. She snagged her bottom lip with her top teeth and gazed up at him like she'd just hit the jackpot.

Emmett cocked one eyebrow, nodded, then continued to scan the room for Liam.

He found him down the hallway on the phone, with no woman on his arm or waiting in the wings for him. Interesting.

"Ready, everyone?" Daisy chirruped, wrapping her arm around Riley.

Riley wrapped his arm around his wife and gazed down

at her with all the love in the world. They held their champagne flutes in their free hands and, with the rest of the crowd, began to count down.

"Ten ... nine ... eight ... seven ... "

A couple of the women around Emmett and Mason inched closer to them. Emmett fought the urge to roll his eyes. Mason just smiled wider and pecked the top of Willow's head.

"Four ... three ... two ... one! Happy New Year!" The entire house erupted into hoots and hollers, whoops and cheers.

Music began to play, people clapped, and suddenly everyone around Emmett and Mason was kissing.

"Ah, come here, you dumbass," Mason said, grabbing Emmett around the back of the head and, before Emmett could pull away, planting a big, smacking, closed-mouth smooch onto his lips.

Emmett was stunned. So were all the women around them. Their gasps, groans and then murmurs of "of course, all the good ones left are gay" filtered in through the continuous celebration.

Mason finally released Emmett and pulled away.

Emmett glared at him. Mason just smiled even wider.

"Dude," Emmett said, wiping his mouth, "not cool. Love is love and all that shit, but not cool."

Mason rolled his eyes before leaning over. "Did you want to kiss any of those does in estrus?"

He grimaced. "No."

His friend shrugged. "Neither did I. Got my eye on a cutie who keeps coming to the bar and interviewing guys. It's fucking bizarre, but when we started to count down, she was the only person I could think of that I even wanted to remotely kiss. Knew I couldn't kiss anybody else." He bobbed his eyebrows and then lifted his hand to cup Emmett's cheek, gazing at him lovingly. "Well, besides you, handsome."

Emmett batted his friend's hand away. "You're a dork."

"A dork you find irresistible." Mason's eyes turned soft and he made to cup Emmett's face again, but Emmett ducked his advances.

Mason hadn't mentioned a new woman on his radar though. The man was so deep in new-dad mode and work, Emmett didn't think he had time to date.

The ruckus in the living room began to die down. Liam was up at the bar now, his phone no longer glued to his ear, and he was ordering a drink from the bartender. Mason and Emmett climbed the few steps out of the sunken living room.

"Who were you on the phone with?" Mason asked, ordering a beer from the bartender.

Liam shook his head. "Just ... nobody." He sipped his scotch.

Emmett and Mason exchanged knowing glances. Liam had been on the phone with Richelle. There wasn't anybody else out there he would have dismissed speaking to. The question was: Did Liam call her, or did she call him?

"Where's Zara?" Liam asked, his eyes scanning the living room. "Didn't see you two sucking face a moment ago." He pointed at Mason and Emmett. "Saw *you two* sucking face but figured that was just to avoid random lips."

Mason tapped his nose to indicate Liam was on the money with his assumption.

"Zara left with her son about an hour ago," Emmett said, thanking the bartender for his rye and tonic and immediately taking a big, long sip.

Liam's brown eyes narrowed. "You drive her off?" His face fell, his infamous Dixon smile disappearing. "Fuck, did *I* drive her off?" He looked truly remorseful.

Emmett shook his head. "No, I drove her off. We reconciled after your oversharing earlier, and she gave me another chance. We actually ... " He cleared his throat. "In the wine cellar earlier. But then I started to get squirrelly when she was trying to make nice with JoJo. I just don't want to confuse my kid."

Now it was Liam and Mason's turn to exchange glances.

"You do tend to get squirrelly," Liam agreed. "You need to loosen up. Zara seemed like a really nice woman—one I would consider dumping your ass for as a client and representing her instead of you in your inevitable divorce." His smile turned mischievous as Emmett's glare darkened. But true to form, Liam couldn't give two shits that he'd offended Emmett and just kept on talking. "So what if she met your kid already? She's got a kid too, right? And you met him, and she didn't get all squirrelly on you."

Emmett nodded. "Yeah, Nolan. I cleaned up the cut on his head after he fell on the stairs. And he comforted JoJo earlier when some girls downstairs were mean to her. He's a great kid."

"Because he's got a great mom," Mason added. "Honestly, dude, if I wasn't hung up on this mystery chick at the bar, I'd be hitting on Zara. However, I don't know if I want to wreck my relationship with my florist. Where would I go if the relationship went south? Pike Place Posies? *Pffst,* no. Zara knows exactly what my mom likes. The relationship between a man and his florist is sacred. I don't know if I could jeopardize that by sleeping with her."

Both Liam and Emmett snorted.

The relationship between a man and his florist is sacred.

What the fuck?

They stepped to the side so other people could sidle up to the bar and order drinks.

Willow began to stir in the carrier, and Liam perked up, drained his scotch and made *gimme* hands. "Gimme that little chick magnet," he said, waiting for Mason to pull her sleepy little body from the carrier. Once she was free, she stretched, made goofy faces, yawned and blinked a bunch.

There was no doubt about it, Willow was an adorable baby. Mason must have had a gorgeous egg donor.

Liam took Willow and held her against his chest. "Hey, baby. It's your Uncle Liam. The smartest and best-looking of all your uncles." He kissed the top of her head and rested his nose against her hair, letting his eyes gently close.

Anti-love? Sure.

Anti-commitment? Sure.

Anti-feelings?

Anti-compassion?

Anti-loyalty?

Anti-sensitivity?

Anti-baby?

No freaking way.

Liam was a lot of things. An asshole from time to time. A jaded jerk. A loudmouth pain. But he was also a tremendous human being at the root of it all, and one of the few human beings on the planet that Emmett would not only trust his life with, but also his daughters.

Liam kissed the top of Willow's head again. "There, that's my New Year's Eve kiss. I'm the luckiest man in the house." Then he wandered off with Willow snuggled tightly in his arms, taking in the admiring glances of all the women but not really biting at their advances.

He could sing it from the rooftops that he didn't have feelings for Richelle, but Liam Dixon was a loyal man, and even if they weren't serious or exclusive, he would never step out on her in a million years.

The man oozed integrity from every pore in his body. That was the main reason Emmett continued to put up with the man's idiosyncrasies and annoying ways. Liam Dixon— for all his faults—had more integrity in his pinky finger than most people had in their entire bodies. And to Emmett, integrity was everything.

"So, care to share more about your fuckup?" Mason asked, tipping back his beer and giving Emmett the ol' side eye.

Emmett exhaled and lifted up the giraffe still in his other hand. "Her son forgot his favorite stuffed animal. Do you think I should go over to her house, drop it off—"

"And apologize for being a tight-ass?" Mason interrupted. "Yes, yes, I do. Because you are, and it sounds like you were."

Emmett nodded. "I was. I knew the moment it happened what I was doing, but for some reason, I couldn't turn it off. It's so ingrained in who I am. A stickler to the rules. Rules are meant to be followed. Rules are what keep us safe."

"Rules are meant to be revisited, revised and sometimes even broken," Mason challenged. "I know you want to protect Josie, and honestly, dude, you are raising that little girl right, but you need to back off and let her skin her knees. Let her figure out the world for herself to some extent. Don't be a helicopter parent."

He'd been accused of being a helicopter parent by his friends before. Whenever they'd go to the park, he was usually right up on the play structures with JoJo, making sure she didn't fall, holding her hand when she went down the slide, hovering beneath her when she climbed the jungle gym.

"She's freaking five years old and better on the monkey bars than you are, dude," Mitch often said. "Just let her be." Meanwhile his daughter, Jayda, who was already six, was dangling upside down from the top of the jungle gym and Mitch was cheering her on.

Even the thought of his Josie doing such a thing made an enormous pit form in Emmett's stomach.

He just couldn't bear it if his little girl got hurt. Her body or her heart.

And if he could in any way prevent either from happening and didn't, he wasn't sure he'd ever be able to forgive himself.

"Listen," Mason continued, "I know my kid is only four months old and I'm not divorced, but I've been watching all you dads for a few months now, learning and observing. Mark's kid, Adam's kid, Mitch's kid they are all doing really well. They're happy kids.

"Their fathers are happy, and the women their fathers are with are amazing with the children. It's all worked out ... " He scratched the back of his neck. "I mean *so far*. But I honestly don't see any of those relationships tanking. What is so bad about bending the rules if it makes everybody involved happy?"

Because as he knew firsthand with his own marriage, that happiness could be fleeting. You could think things were great one minute, all of you laughing and playing on a family vacation to San Diego, then suddenly you're being served with divorce papers two weeks later.

"Zara's not Tiff," Mason said, his blue eyes turning serious. "And if it doesn't work out, then yeah, it'll be hard on JoJo, but she's a tough kid, and she will get over it. But I wouldn't push away something good, deny yourself joy, because you're worried something bad might happen in the future."

Emmett took a long sip of his rye, his gaze circling the room. As much as the party was still going full force, it felt less vibrant, less alive without Zara. She had an undeniable spark that just seemed to add a glow to the room. He hardly knew the woman, and yet, in the short amount of time he'd spent with her, he knew there was something really special about her. A calmness he so desperately needed in his life.

She was bright and funny and beautiful, classically so. She didn't need to put on airs and slather herself in product to look gorgeous. Her makeup and hair had been tasteful, her dress beautiful and classy. She was a classy woman all around, and he'd simply turned out to be a class-A jerk.

"I mean, if we all operated under that ridiculous logic," Mason went on, "we'd never get married, never have kids. Hell, we'd never get our driver's licenses or go on planes. We'd all wander around encased in bubble wrap with a tool belt of super glue and duct tape." He snickered at his own joke, shaking his head. "Though duct tape can fix just about anything."

Emmett wasn't really listening anymore. He was still mulling over what Mason had said before. The truth of it hit Emmett right upside the head.

I wouldn't push away something good, deny yourself joy, because you're worried something bad might happen in the future.

Mason was right. Emmett was so worried about another relationship ending abruptly and hurting JoJo's heart again— and if he was being honest, his heart too—that he was denying both of them—all of them—the possibility of solid, meaningful relationships. Of a new beginning, a happily ever after.

Worrying about all the negative *what ifs,* he was ignoring all the positive *what could bes.* He was letting his past scars impact his future, impact his healing.

He glanced up at Mason. "JoJo's asleep in the guest room down the hall. Can you—"

Mason held up his hand and nodded. "Say no more, bro. I got your back. Liam and Scott are here too. And I'm sure JoJo knows Daisy and Riley enough to not freak out if she wakes up and you're not here."

Fuck, Emmett loved his brotherhood of single fathers. They really did have each other's backs.

He finished his drink, slapped Mason on the shoulder and thanked him. Then he took off, with Ziggy the giraffe safely in his hand, to go find Daisy and get an address.

He wasn't going to let Zara get away. He certainly wasn't going to waste the night or start the new year off without getting to at least apologize, at least explain himself. He needed to let the incredible woman who appreciated a good everything bagel with cream cheese, lox and cucumbers know he wasn't above growth and change. He just needed a good woman by his side to help him—to be worth changing for. And he knew—even in the short time he'd known her—that Zara was that kind of a good woman.

He'd known it all along. He'd just been blinded by his desperate need to protect JoJo's heart.

And your own heart. Kids are excellent scapegoats, but let's start the new year off with honesty.

Fine. Yes, his heart too. He was jaded and still recovering from the epic burn by his ex. He'd been in self-preservation mode and had unfortunately gone about it all wrong. Now he needed to right his wrongs, turn back the clock and see if Zara would be willing to start the night over.

11

ZARA YAWNED, tipped her wine glass back and finished it. The clock on the wall in the living room said it was one thirty. With strained ears and an open window, she thought she could sort of hear celebrations going on outside earlier, but they could have been coming from anywhere in the neighborhood, not necessarily a couple of blocks away at Daisy's house.

Was Emmett still there?

Had he found someone to kiss?

Probably.

Unable to go to sleep, she bounced back and forth between channels, watching a stupid teen rom-com on the movie channel and then flicking to Times Square during the commercials.

Maybe this year her son would start sleeping in. One could only hope. Since he was a baby, Nolan would wake with the sun, bouncing into her room with a big smile and bright eyes, asking when they could start the day.

Even when he went to bed late, her son was an early riser.

She didn't want to wish her kid's childhood away, but she

was looking forward to the teen years when all they did was sleep.

And eat.

Oh God, her grocery bills were going to be through the roof. Maybe she should think about franchising the flower shop?

Yawning again and dreading the thought of being up in six hours or less to make pancakes, she retracted the footstool on her recliner and rose from her chair.

"*Alexa,* turn off the television, please."

She paused, waited and then snorted.

She had no Alexa. She *was* Alexa.

"*Turning off the television,*" she said in her best female robot voice, clicking the off button on the remote and taking her wine glass to the kitchen.

Maybe she should get an Alexa. It'd be like having a partner in the house who picked up the slack but didn't make her feel like crap or unwelcome. She could program Alexa to greet her when she walked in the door, ask about her day, order takeout if Zara didn't feel like cooking.

Besides the lack of affection and intimacy and a decent foot rub during wedding flower season, Alexa actually seemed like the perfect companion.

Did they make a male version of Alexa? *Alex*? Could she program him to talk dirty to her as she used her vibrator? Was that weird? Was that taking the whole AI thing too far?

Contemplating the idea of a robot boyfriend and how she could get her hands on one, she kept her bandaged hand dry and rinsed out her wine glass with her good hand, then placed it in the drying rack.

She removed her great grandmother's earrings, her grandmother's ring and her mother's necklace, then went to double-check that the front door was locked. She normally never did it, but for some reason she was compelled to peer through the peephole.

She nearly had a coronary when she saw a man standing on the welcome mat.

She pulled back and spun around, plastering her back to the door, her heart thumping wildly in her chest. She placed her finger to the pulse in her neck.

"Deep breaths. Deep, deep breaths," she whispered.

Where was her phone? Should she call the police?

Where was her baseball bat? Probably in the garage. She wouldn't have time to run and grab it. What else could she use as an immediate weapon?

Her eyes scanned her small, narrow foyer and landed on Nolan's child-size green froggy umbrella tucked next to the shoe rack. It would have to do. She lunged for it and clutched it against her chest just as a gentle, barely discernible knock rapped the door behind her. "Zara?" came a low, masculine voice. "Are you awake? It's Emmett."

Emmett!

She turned back around and peered back through the peephole. He'd taken a couple of steps back so she could now see him. His cheeks were a rosy red, his eyes bright and a touch watery, and snow flurries dusted the shoulders of his peacoat and his hair.

Had he walked to her house?

Should she pretend she was already in bed? Not answer and wait until he turned around and left?

She squinted back through the peephole.

"I brought Nolan's giraffe," he said, holding it up. "JoJo was awfully upset when she realized he left it behind."

Deliberately left it behind.

"Why are you *really* here, Emmett?" she asked through the door, still watching him.

He lifted his head and stared directly at her as if he could see her through the peephole. His mouth twitched as if trying to smile. "I brought Nolan his giraffe. If he's anything like JoJo, I figured maybe he might not be able to go to sleep without him."

Oh.

Her face fell, and she took a step away from the door, setting the umbrella back down on the floor.

"I also came here to see you. To talk to you."

Oh!

Her chest slammed the door again, and she shut one eye to see him better through the small hole.

He swallowed, shoved his hands into his pockets and shivered.

The wind whipped flurries around behind him. It had started to snow again as Zara and Nolan were getting into the house. She didn't think snow was in the forecast, but then those meteorologists were only ever fifty percent right. Some less than that.

Her ex-husband was a meteorologist.

She didn't give them much credit.

Didn't trust them.

And for good reason.

"Zara?"

She blinked, placed her palms on the door and peered back through the peephole at Emmett.

"You still there?"

Exhaling, she pulled her face away from the door and reached for the knob. With a pause and a moment of self-talk, she unlocked the door and opened it.

"I'm still here," she whispered, coming face to face with a man she'd known for less than a day but in that time had allowed to take a small piece of her heart and then shatter it.

She really needed to stop wearing her heart on her sleeve.

She was forty-four years old. She was done with dumb men and their bullshit.

She took a step back and welcomed him into the foyer, shivering as a gust of icy wind followed him in.

She stepped around him, careful not to get too close, and shut the door. Then, before she could let him get into her space, she turned around and walked into the kitchen, grabbing her long handmade shawl off the back of a kitchen chair and draping it around her shoulders.

She hadn't expected him to follow her, but when she lifted her head, he was right there, standing in front of her, close enough that she felt the need to take a half-step back.

He smelled like his incredible self, rye and snow. The combination of it all made her sway where she stood—or perhaps it was the nearly full bottle of wine she'd just consumed. Either way, she reached out and gripped the back of the chair to keep herself steady.

His throat undulated on a hard swallow, and he lifted his arm, handing her Ziggy. His eyes followed his hand until their gazes locked. Unease swirled behind the bright amber, and a rush of heat flooded his already very pink cheeks. "I came here to apologize for earlier," he said, clearing his throat. "I was an asshole, and I'm really sorry."

She took Ziggy from him, then wrapped herself up even tighter in her shawl. "Yes, you were," she said, making sure to keep her tone even. "One minute you're complimenting me on my son, the next you're giving me the evil eye for talking to your daughter, making me think that the only reason you said the first thing was to get me to have sex with you. *Compliment her parenting and she'll let you use your trusty pocket condom.*"

Anger infused her tone. She needed to take it down a couple of notches, drop her voice a few octaves and lower her volume. The last thing she wanted to do was wake Nolan.

The poor kid would probably think his ploy to leave Ziggy behind had worked and Emmett was there to take them all out for breakfast.

Ha!

Fat chance of that.

He opened his mouth to say something, but she cut him off. She wasn't finished reading him the riot act. If he came over here to *talk,* first, he was going to listen. She was going to say all the things she couldn't say earlier because their children were around. "What did you think I was going to do, Emmett? What threat do I pose to Josie? To you? Did you think I was going to tell your kid we had sex in the wine cellar and then ask if I could be her new mommy?"

His eyes went wide, and his mouth dropped open.

Zara took a few step back and leaned against the stove, crossing her arms over her chest and her legs at the ankles. She needed him to think she was over him already, that he hadn't hurt her the way he had. That she was unaffected by his behavior, besides maybe being put off and unimpressed.

"I don't have time for bullshit," she finally said, having paused just long enough to make him squirm where he stood. She enjoyed seeing him uncomfortable. It was how she had felt when he was treating her like a wad of gum on the bottom of his shoe earlier.

He nodded. "I know. And I'm sorry. I never said those things to you just to get you to have sex with me. I would never do such a thing. I meant what I said, I swear."

She scoffed, her head shaking, her arms still crossed. "You're going to have to do a lot better than just *I'm sorry*. You may have all these rules about people meeting your kid, but sometimes life doesn't go exactly how we plan it. Life doesn't always *follow the rules*." She threw her hands up in the air. "Hell, you think when I was twenty, I *planned* to get married to man who didn't want to have children with me, divorce him, and then have a child with my gay best friend? No. But we roll with it. We play the hand we're dealt and make the best of it."

"I'm learning that I need to be more flexible. That I need to embrace fate and not try to control everything. Sometimes rules are meant to be revisited, revised or even broken."

Well, now they were getting somewhere.

He shoved his hands back in his pockets and rocked backward on his heels. "I use JoJo as a cover. I say I'm protecting her heart, protecting her from confusion and heartache, when I'm also protecting myself."

Well, she could have told him that. But instead of playing the *know-it-all* card, she smiled grimly and nodded. "You mentioned you were burned. I get that you're jaded and gun-shy."

He snorted. "That's an understatement. I was blindsided. I had no idea anything was wrong. We'd gone for a great family vacation to San Diego two weeks earlier. I thought things were perfect. Then she served me with divorce papers. Said I was unbearable to live with, a control freak, a workaholic, and that she'd fallen out of love with me."

Oh God.

Even if that was all true, what a horrible thing to say to somebody. Even as much as Emmett had hurt her, Zara would never say such terrible things to him—to anybody.

"It gutted me. I loved Tiff. Loved our life. Our family. I didn't see it coming." He raked his fingers through his hair and broke eye contact. "I mean, why didn't she come to me with her concerns? Why didn't she suggest counseling? I'm not above changing. I'm not above learning and growing. If I love someone, I will be a better person for them." Tears filled his eyes. "She'd been having what *my* counselor called 'an emotional affair' with a man from the dermatology clinic she used to work at. Tiff claims they never acted on anything but that they both planned to leave their spouses. He left his wife at the same time Tiff left me. They were together for a while, and then he went back to his wife."

She took a step forward and tugged on his arm, encouraging him to pull his hands free from his pockets. She knew he needed a physical connection to ground him. She did too. She held his hand in hers. "That's terrible. I am so sorry. Did she try to come back to you?"

He shook his head. "No. A part of me thought she might come back, and that same part considered taking her back ... a *small* part. I know I wasn't the *best* husband in the world. I worked a lot of crazy hours until I became an attending. But I didn't think I was the worst husband either. I was crazy romantic, attentive, complimentary, and willing to change, to learn and do better. But when she didn't come crawling back, I slipped into a really dark state for a while."

"Understandable. When I found out my ex-husband was having a baby with the waitress he met at Chili's, I was devastated. He didn't want children with me, but he did with her? I thought there was something wrong with me. Something unmotherly that he saw inside me that I couldn't, that he didn't think I'd be a fit mother." She nibbled on her bottom lip, and her gaze slid sideways as she fought back the tears. She too had gone to a dark place after she found out Marcello and Tobi were expecting. She questioned her whole life, every choice she'd ever made and whether she really was meant to be a mother. She gulped, still unable to look at him. "I had those feelings again after the way you treated me. Those thoughts came back." Her breath stuttered out of her and she choked on a laugh, blinking back the tears as she shook her head. "I mean I really shouldn't let the opinion of man I've known for less than a day affect me the way it did, but ..." she lifted her gaze to his and shrugged, "I thought we had a connection. I gave you more credit, more power than I should have, and that's *my* fault." She looked away again and sniffed, wiping the back of her wrist beneath her nose.

He tugged on her hand until she brought her gaze back to his face. "Fuck, Zara. Oh God, no. You are so motherly." He ran his hand back through his hair. "I am so sorry. Nolan is so loved, so happy and healthy, so well-adjusted and kind. The way he took care of JoJo—I meant it when I said he is the type of guy I hope JoJo brings home to meet me one day. And that's because of you and how amazing of a mother you are. Your ex was and *is* an idiot for not having children with you."

She squeezed her back teeth together as tight as she could to stop herself from crumpling to the ground in a heap of tears. She was stronger than the weak mess she currently felt like. She was a strong-ass single mom, entrepreneur for Christ's sake. She was standing up to Emmett and letting him know that how he'd treated her was totally unacceptable, she was challenging him just like Daisy said she should. And yet, even now, after all these years, she couldn't let go of those horrible feelings of inadequacy. All that self-doubt. That there was something unmotherly and wrong with her. And those thoughts always brought out the tears. No matter how far she'd come, no matter how strong she was, when those thoughts and feelings invaded her, they took over.

Emmett's hand tightened around hers. "Your ex, he lost out big time. I'm sorry if how I acted made you second-guess yourself as a mother. I never meant that at all. And you should never, ever second-guess how incredible and accomplished you are in raising that boy. You have done and continue to do a phenomenal job with him."

A tear slipped down her cheek, and she sniffed. "Thank you. I needed to hear that." A rattled exhale escaped her and her shoulders dropped away from her ears.

"You're a remarkable person, Zara. Truly."

There was the man she'd met earlier that day, the man

who had mended her hand, made her laugh and kissed her like she was the answer to all his problems.

He let out a huffed exhale. She could tell he had more to say, had more he needed to get off his chest. Though it was a struggle to lift the corners of her mouth, she did the best she could and gave him a reassuring smile so he knew he could continue and she would hear him out.

His own smile was grim but thankful. "I think JoJo saw what the divorce did to me," he continued, "and it made her coping with it harder. She was angry with her mom for a while. Didn't want to stay with her. And it's not like I fueled that. I have never and will never say a negative thing about my ex-wife to or around my daughter. I am very, *very* careful about that."

"Kids are incredibly intuitive, though," she whispered. "Nolan picks up on vibes and moods even before I do."

He nodded, staring at their knotted hands. "JoJo too. She hates Tiff's new boyfriend, and I don't know if that's because she's still dealing with everything or if the guy is a legitimate tool. I don't know him well enough to truly make that call." He lifted his gaze back up to hers. "I know I have control issues. And I'm working on them. I know that I *can't* control everything that happens in life or every situation. And that sometimes the best-laid plans go completely out the window and I need to learn to be okay with that." He swallowed again, his own eyes once again growing watery. "I'm still a work in progress"—he shrugged, and a half smile picked up the corner of his mouth—"but aren't we all?"

She lifted a shoulder and nodded.

In some ways, she agreed. Yes, they were all a constant work in progress. At least those in society who strived for continuous growth and self-improvement. But at the same time, you kind of hoped you didn't have to deal with a complete mess once you were in your forties. You hoped any man you dated or started a relationship with had his shit together and his moods sorted out.

She was not looking for a project.

Could he see that all on her face?

He must have, because the next words that came out were filled with not only hope but also fear.

"I understand if you're not interested in taking on a risk like me. And I don't blame you. I'm still sorting out this single dad thing, still trying to figure out where I went wrong in my marriage." Now it was his turn to lift his shoulders. "I honestly thought I'd done everything right with Tiff."

She wasn't interested in hearing about his ex or their divorce. She was also exhausted.

"But I just had to come here and tell you that I'm really sorry for how I treated you and that it had nothing to do with you." He snorted. "In this case, I can honestly say, *it's not you, it's me.*"

Zara snickered and dipped her head for a moment before lifting her gaze once again to his face. "Yeah, it really was you."

His mouth jiggled at one corner.

She could tell he was really trying. And hadn't Daisy said he was not above self-improvement or change? That he was a man who always strived to become a better version of himself?

Maybe he just needed something—or someone—to be the incentive.

"Come with me." She led him into her living room, leaving the lights off, though the light over the stove in the kitchen lent enough of a glow to the room that she could still make out his handsome face.

"I wasn't trying to push getting to know Josie," she said, intertwining their fingers together and pulling him down with her so they could sit on the couch. "If you have rules about people getting acquainted with your daughter, then I respect that. But given the circumstances, I didn't think what I was doing was that bad."

"It wasn't," he said plainly. "I was overreacting like an overprotective, helicopter nut-job parent."

She nodded. "Yes, you were."

"The guys call me *the helicopter* when we're at the park. Make rotor noises and spin their fingers in the air."

She huffed a laugh through her nose. "Maybe they're on to something? A little bit of freedom isn't a bad thing. As long as that freedom has some boundaries."

His head bobbed. "I'm coming to understand that ... albeit slowly."

"Please know that I would never force you to make me a part of her life ... if things between us progressed. Just like I hope you would never force me to make you a dominant presence in Nolan's life. Our kids come first."

"Always. I would take all my cues from you."

"And I would take all my cues from you. But given that we met at a party where our children were and they became fast friends, I figured a few of those rules could be modified at least temporarily."

His mouth dipped into a slight frown before he spoke. "You're right. I should have been more flexible. I just ... "

"You were blinded by hurt. Your heart's and Josie's."

He nodded, released one of her hands and scrubbed his hand down his tired-looking face, pulling on his scruff-covered chin. "Maybe I'm too far gone. Maybe I'm too big of a risk. It's only been eighteen months."

She shrugged. "There's no rule that says how long you need to wait. The same goes for grieving, and although your ex didn't die, in a way you are grieving. You're grieving the loss of your marriage, the loss of your perfect little family unit. A loss is a loss, and we all mourn in our own way." She ran her thumb over the back of his hand, and he lifted his eyes back up to hers. "It all depends on how you *feel*. How do you *feel*?"

He released his chin and took her hand back. "I feel like I want to get to know you. Like I want to see you again, take you out, call you and see where this connection takes us."

"I wanted that too," she said softly.

His eyes turned sad, which made her want to pull him close and hug him. Comfort him through his confusion and frustration. But she couldn't. She still needed to lay a few things out on the table before they got to their discussion of the *future*.

"*Wanted*?" he asked. "You don't feel that anymore?"

As much as he seemed like a project she wasn't interested in taking on, she kept their fingers intertwined and had to repeatedly shove down the urge to lunge across the couch and kiss him. She had this visceral pull to Emmett, an attraction she hadn't felt in ages. He had some real goodness inside him, kindness. The way he'd taken care of Nolan after his fall had melted her heart. He truly cared about people. He was just still hurting inside. And she knew what that felt like firsthand. Marcello had ripped her heart out too, and it'd taken a few years for her to jump back into the dating pool and try again. Yes, Emmett was a risk to her heart, to Nolan's heart, but was he a risk she was willing to take?

Could she give him another chance?

Did she want to?

Yes, she did.

She was willing to take the risk. She just had to make sure she protected her son's heart as best she could in case things didn't work out. She would shield her son from heartache, even if it meant her heart shattered in the process.

Fate had thrown Zara and Emmett together four times in one day. She had to take that as a sign she was meant to see where things went with Dr. Emmett Strong, that he was worth getting to know, worth giving a second chance.

She held her breath for a moment before letting it out through her nose and squeezing his fingers in hers. "I do like you, Emmett. And for a while, I had a lot of fun tonight. But I can't deal with the hot and cold. I'm too old for the drama. If things with your ex are still messy, I can't get involved. I have a business to run, a son to raise and a mortgage to pay. I can deal with you and your growth, but I can't deal with the hot and cold and the extraneous variables like crazy exes."

His mouth spread into a small smile. "Me either. And I promise, Tiff won't be a problem. We're getting to be on better terms. It's slow, but it is getting better. And I will definitely try to keep my temperature in check, no more—"

"Surface of the sun to sub-zero?" she interrupted.

His smile grew. "No more surface of the sun to sub-zero. You've met JoJo, and she really likes you. She likes Nolan. I'd love it if the four of us grabbed breakfast—"

She hadn't been able to stop herself, and she yawned again.

He chuckled. "Or *lunch*, if you need to sleep. But I'd love it if the four of us grabbed a bite later today. The kids really hit it off, and up until JoJo's father made a complete ass of himself, their parents seemed to really hit it off too."

"We'll take it slow," she said, inching closer to him on the couch until their knees touched. "We won't go crazy with the kids, making them a fixture in our"—she pointed back and forth between them—"whatever this is. But brunch tomorrow sounds lovely."

"I really am sorry, Zara. I will do better, I promise." He grimaced. "That is, if you'll *let* me do better. If you'll let me show you I'm not this raging lunatic who's a charmer one minute and a jackass the next. I am actually a nice guy, I just ... "

She peeled her butt off the couch and crawled into his lap, looping her arms around his neck. "Daisy said you handle your anger by going to The Rage Room. Would you take me sometime? I'd love to smash the shit out of some vases."

His eyebrows shot up into his hairline, but he visibly relaxed the moment she was in his arms. "Isn't that sacrilege for a florist?" His fingers made trails of magic along her spine.

She bent her head until they were nose to nose, their breaths mingling, her bandaged hand over his broken heart. Could she help mend his heart just like he'd helped mend her hand? "It is, but I think the florist gods would forgive me."

"Do you forgive me?" His hand paused on her back, and he pulled away from her face just enough to really look deep into her eyes.

She grinned. "That depends ... "

He squinted. "On what?"

"On how you answer the next three questions."

He took a deep breath and nodded. "I'll do my best."

"Okay then. One: Where is your ideal vacation? Two: top quality you look for in a good friend or partner? And three: If you could sit down with any person from your past and ask them one question, who would it be and what would you ask?"

Emmett let out a breath slowly through his mouth. "Those are good questions. I'd have to say, Hawaii, integrity and my grandfather, Emmett, who I was named after. And I would ask him for his secret to a happy and healthy marriage. He and my grandmother met in grade school and were married for forty years before he passed away. I never got the chance to meet him, but according to everyone, he was one heck of a guy."

Zara's eyes flared, and her smile stretched across her mouth.

"Did I pass?" he asked with a lopsided smile of hesitation, his brows knitting together.

"With flying colors." She glanced at the clock on the wall. It was thirty seconds to two o'clock. "In about twenty-five seconds, Hawaii is going to be celebrating the new year," she murmured. "Care to be my Hawaiian new year's kiss?"

His grin made her heart skip a beat. "That depends. Are you all right ringing in the new year with just little ol' me? Dr. Emmett Strong? Because Officer Astronaut Dr. Emmett Strong is a bit of a jerk."

"I prefer little ol' Dr. Emmett Strong any day. In fact, I really like him." Her heart skipped another beat. She glanced back up at the clock and began counting. "Fifteen ... fourteen ... thirteen ... twelve ... "

The fingers of his free hand cupped her face, and she leaned into his touch, grateful to be there once again and that Emmett was the man she thought he was the first time they met, not the man she'd left at the party wondering how she could have completely misjudged someone.

"There's no one I'd rather ring in Hawaii's new year with," he whispered.

"Me either. Eight ... seven." She gripped the lapel of his coat and tugged him closer so once again they breathed each other in.

"Five ... four—Ah, fuck it." Then he took her mouth with his, fully and completely, and together they celebrated the new year two hours late ... but for them, it was right on time.

12

"IT'S SO NOISY IN HERE," JoJo said with a yawn, stabbing a chunk of scrambled egg with her fork and bringing it to her mouth. "Why couldn't we go to Aunt Paige's restaurant?" She wrinkled her nose and glared at the table of lively college kids probably still drunk from their night out club-hopping and ringing in the new year.

"Because Aunt Paige's bistro is closed, honey," Emmett said, taking a long, much-needed sip of his coffee. After he and Zara had kissed and rung in the new year with Hawaii, he'd taken her to her bed and apologized properly for a good hour or more. Then he'd raced back to Riley and Daisy's house, where the party was finally winding down, and he climbed up onto the top bunk in the same room as JoJo and caught a couple of hours of sleep.

Not nearly enough though.

JoJo had woken up only a few hours later from all the noise in the house.

Poor Riley and Daisy were up early with their children. Baby Chelsea was suddenly particularly fussy after a long night, and little Nick had found a noisemaker and was blowing it like a freaking bugle.

So with tired eyes and wrinkled clothing, Emmett and his daughter drove over to Zara's and met her and Nolan. Then the four of them—*all* with tired eyes and yawns aplenty—headed to the Pink Flamingo Diner for breakfast.

"I don't mind the place," Nolan said, having ordered a breakfast fit for a linebacker and making a decent dent in it. "I love their pancakes." He speared an entire pancake and lifted it with his fork, attempting to shove the whole thing into his mouth.

"Ah, ah, ah," Zara said, resting a hand on his arm. "Cut it up, please, mister. You know how to use a knife. Please do so."

Nolan rolled his eyes, put his fork down and grabbed his knife. "Fine."

Emmett hid his smile and laugh in his napkin, wiping his mouth. They were at a busy diner downtown where the portions were generous, the coffee palatable and the décor like an old-fashioned soda shop with the black and white tiled , turquoise plastic booth seats, and a big shiny juke box in the corner. They'd only had to wait forty-five minutes for a table, which for this diner wasn't bad at all, particularly on New Year's Day.

Things in this new year were already looking up.

Finally.

"So, what's your new year's resolution, Nolan?" Emmett asked, having already finished his own breakfast. He dropped his hand down to the seat of the booth and snuck it across the plastic until it found Zara's thigh.

Nolan lifted his head up, his mouth full of pancake. "What's a new year's—" His nose wrinkled in confusion. "Whatever you—"

"Chew, swallow, then speak, please," Zara said, her

bandaged hand once again landing on her son's arm. "We don't speak with our mouths full."

Nolan grumbled, made an ostentatious display of chewing and swallowing, then took a long sip of his chocolate milk. He wiped the back of his wrist over his mouth and let out a loud *Ah* before turning his attention back to Emmett. "What's a new year's ... restitution?"

Emmett grinned. "A new year's *resolution* is something you'd like to do this year, that you didn't do last year. Something you'd like to accomplish or improve on. Like maybe last year you only read twenty books and this year you'd like to read thirty. Or maybe this year instead of taking the elevator, you're going to take the stairs."

"What about last year I only scored three goals the whole soccer season and this year I am going to score fifty?" Nolan asked, using his finger to scoop a big dollop of whipped cream into his mouth.

"Fifty is a *huge* number," JoJo replied, having chosen scrambled eggs, bacon and a strawberry milkshake for her own breakfast. Emmett was too tired to enforce any kind of rules for breakfast. As long as his kid had a full belly, was happy and not losing her shit because she was so tired, he was a happy man. Besides, strawberries were fruit, right? Who cared if they were in the form of a milkshake?

Nolan turned to JoJo. "It is, but that's my new year's reservation."

"Resolution," Zara corrected.

Nolan nodded. "Right. Josie, what's your new year's res-o-lution?"

Picking up a piece of extra-crispy bacon—just the way she liked it—Emmett's daughter pinched her brows in thought. Emmett could practically see the cogs spinning in her head. She finished her bacon and licked her index finger before holding it up in the air. "My new year's res-evolution is that I will try to do one nice thing for someone else every day."

Emmett's heart practically exploded in his chest.

He squeezed Zara's thigh. Her hand landed on his, and she squeezed him back. Her gaze left their children and slowly slid to Emmett until their eyes locked.

Her lip twitched, then his did.

"Ohh," Nolan said, now blowing bubbles in his chocolate milk, "I like that one. Can I do that too?" He turned to face Zara and Emmett, who were now staring deeply into each other's eyes, not saying a word. "Can I have two new year's res-o ... whatever they're called?"

"Yeah," JoJo replied. "You can prolly have like fifty."

"Is JoJo's dad your boyfriend, Mom?" Nolan asked, switching gears faster than a Formula One driver.

Zara's body began to shake, which caused the moment between Emmett and Zara to be broken. He lifted his gaze from the woman he'd fallen hard for and had literally only known for twenty-four hours to find her son shaking her by the shoulder. "Mom, is he your boyfriend?"

Emmett could practically hear Zara swallow next to him. Her hand certainly tensed around his.

"No, they're not. Because boyfriends are *stupid*," JoJo said. "My mom's boyfriend is so stupid."

Where the heck had she learned that word?

"Josephine," Emmett scolded, "we don't use that kind of language. We don't call people stupid."

His daughter's blue eyes shifted down toward her plate. "Sorry, Daddy. But I don't like Huntley. And you're way better than Huntley."

"His name is Huntley?" Zara said under her breath. "Isn't that the dog in Curious George?"

"That dog is pronounced *Hundley*," he replied, keeping his voice just as low as hers. "I made that mistake too."

Zara gave one quick nod. "Oh."

"Yeah, but my dad's boyfriend Shane—who is now my Papa—he wasn't stupid," Nolan countered. "I don't think *all* boyfriends are stupid. Just your mom's." He turned to face JoJo, both of their faces far too serious for their young ages. "I'm sure your dad isn't going to be like Huntley." He made a confused face. "Isn't that the wiener dog from Curious George?"

"That's *Hundley*, honey," Zara corrected.

Nolan didn't seem to care any longer and took another sip of his chocolate milk, his attention now on the snowplow outside.

JoJo still seemed perplexed, though, and she fiddled with her fork in her lap. Emmett stood up from his seat in the booth and moved around to sit next to his daughter, scooting in close to her and taking the fork away from her fidgeting hands. "What's wrong, JoJo-bean?"

She lifted her head and blinked big, exhausted blue eyes at him. "I just don't want you to turn into Huntley."

He wrapped his arm around her and chuckled. "Oh, sweetie. You don't have to worry a bit about that. I will *never* turn into Huntley."

"Promise?" She held out her pinky.

He linked his pinky finger with hers. "I promise."

Her mouth scrunched into a tight pout. "This better not be like your promise to wake me up for the ball dropping. You forgot." Her pinky finger tightened around his and she glared at him. "You promised to wake me up and you didn't."

Yeah, he'd been dealing with that all day. JoJo was not letting him live that blunder down.

He held up his other pinky finger and she immediately linked her other pinky through it. "I'm really sorry about that, JoJo-bean. You were just sleeping so peacefully."

"I bet a slice of mudslide ice cream cake would help me

forgive you faster," she said, her pout morphing into an enormous grin and her eyebrows lifting on her forehead.

"Oh, I like that plan," Nolan chimed in. "Mom, I'm still disappointed that you didn't want me up for the countdown either. Can I have ice cream cake?"

Emmett and Zara both snorted and smiled at their cheeky children.

"Ice cream cake, huh?" he asked, his pinky fingers still linked with JoJo's.

She nodded with wide, eager eyes. "Yeah."

Thankfully, at that moment a waiter passed their table and Emmett flagged him down. "Uh, can we have two," he glanced at Zara for confirmation, and she simply bobbed her head once, "yeah, can we have two slices of mudslide ice cream cake, please."

The kids' gasps had both he and Zara laughing.

"With extra whipped cream, please?"

The waiter nodded then took off toward the kitchen.

Nolan did a fist pump and JoJo released Emmett's fingers and bounced in her seat, her smile enormous and beautiful. "Okay, I forgive you. And you can be Nolan's mommy's boyfriend."

Emmett lifted his head and glanced across the table at Zara, whose eyes glowed with an intensity he knew he'd never get tired of seeing. "Thanks, honey." Then he swiveled around to face Nolan. "What do you say, Nolan? Can I be your mom's boyfriend? Would you be okay with that?"

Nolan made what Emmett would call *the cool guy frown and nod*. "Yeah, I'm cool with that."

Zara snickered where she sat, and Emmett had to keep himself from joining her. Instead, he smiled at the little boy before turning his gaze back to the most beautiful woman in the restaurant. "I'd be pretty cool with that too."

EPILOGUE

Two years later ...

EMMETT TURNED on the oven in his kitchen and then opened his refrigerator, grabbing the mozzarella cheese and bell peppers. The sound of heavy footsteps coming down the stairs told him his sous chef was ready to make pizza.

"Hands are washed," Nolan said, bouncing into the kitchen and clapping twice before grabbing an apron off the hook next to the pantry. "Can I use the big knife to cut up the peppers and mushrooms?"

Emmett nodded. "Sure, buddy. I'll grate the cheese and prep the pizza dough with the sauce. You do the chopping."

"Mom and Josie are going to get us the special lunchmeat, right?"

Emmett nodded again. "Right."

Nolan sidled up next to Emmett at the counter and grabbed the cutting board from the cupboard above his head, then pulled the drawer open and brought out the super-sharp knife. "I like it when it's just us sometimes," he said, opening up the brown bag of mushrooms that Emmett had already placed on the counter and beginning to carefully slice them.

Emmett smiled and glanced over at the young man he'd gotten to know quite well over the last two years. It hadn't taken much effort to love Nolan. The kid was a truly decent and upstanding person all around. Zara and Michael were doing a tremendous job as parents. "I like it when it's just us sometimes too," he finally said. "Especially now, because I wanted to ask you something."

Nolan lifted his eyebrows but didn't bother shifting his glance sideways at all. "Yeah, what's that?" In addition to sprouting a good five inches, Nolan had also grown *cool* in the last couple of years, and at nine years old now, his mannerisms were becoming quite hilarious.

Emmett began grating the mozzarella, trying hard not to smile too big. "Well, your mom and I have been together for a couple of years now."

"Mhmm."

"And I really love her."

"I know."

"And I think she really loves me."

"She does."

Emmett rolled his eyes and smiled again, continuing to keep his focus on the cheese grater. "And I love you. JoJo loves you. We work well together, the four of us."

"Yep."

Shit, was this what they had to look forward to in the teenage years? These one- and two-word responses? Gah. Was he like this as a teenager? No wonder his mother constantly threatened to ship him off to military school if he didn't start speaking in complete sentences and engaging in conversation with her.

He needed to get this kid talking. "Well, what do you think of the idea of your mom and I getting married?"

Nolan paused his chopping.

Shit, maybe Emmett shouldn't have asked the kid that question while he was wielding a potential weapon.

Nolan's gaze slid sideways, then he slowly pivoted his body to face Emmett's. "Have you asked her?" he finally asked. Emmett was unable to gauge the young man's expression. Nolan was deliberately keeping his face blank.

Emmett swallowed and shook his head. "No, I haven't. Not yet." He relaxed his shoulders, then dug into his jeans pocket and brought out the jewelry box. He handed it to Nolan. "Actually, I wanted to ask for your permission first. I wanted to make sure you were okay with the idea before I asked your mom. Your opinion matters here too. Your feelings are just as important. We're all in this together."

"Does Josie know you want to marry my mom?" He took the ring box from Emmett but didn't bother to open it.

Once again, Emmett shook his head. "No. JoJo has a bit of a hard time still keeping secrets. I asked her in a roundabout way what she would think about Zara and I getting married, and all she could think about was the fact that then she'd have a big brother, and she was very excited."

Finally, Nolan smiled. It was a big smile, a genuine smile, a smile that usually only came out when JoJo made him laugh—which was a lot.

The two were the best of friends. Brother and sister without even trying.

"I love Josie," he said. He opened the ring box. His eyebrows lifted just a touch. "And I love you too." He lifted his eyes from the ring to Emmett's face. "I'm okay if you and my mom get married." He closed the ring box and passed it back to Emmett. "Mom will like the ring."

Phew.

Emmett was about to thank Nolan and remind him that this was a secret when the front door opened. Then before

Emmett could grab his soon-to-be stepson to let him know that he planned to pop the question to Zara that night when the ball dropped and they all rang in the new year, Nolan dropped the knife and mushroom to the cutting board and took off in the direction of the door. "Mom!"

Shit!

Emmett took off after him.

It was too late though.

"Mom, you can marry Emmett. I just told him I'm okay with it. So you guys can get married and then Josie and I will be brother and sister."

JoJo gasped, her blue eyes going buggy, her smile even wider. "Really?"

Zara dropped the two fabric grocery bags she was holding.

Thank goodness she hadn't had eggs on the shopping list.

Her own blue eyes, eyes Emmett loved, eyes Emmett would never get tired of waking up to or staring into every day, went wide and her soft, full lips parted. "Nolan, what are you talking about?" Her gaze shifted to Emmett.

"Emmett just asked me if he could ask you to marry him and I said yes. So when he asks you, you can say yes. Because I said yes." He reached into one of the grocery bags and pulled out a bunch of bananas. "I hope you remembered the chocolate and strawberry syrup. A banana split will just be bananas and ice cream without them." He took off in the direction of the kitchen, completely oblivious to the bomb he'd just dropped.

JoJo reached into the same grocery bag and grabbed two bottles of syrup. "We did get the syrup, see? Are you helping my dad make pizza? We bought the lunch meat."

Their chatter faded into the kitchen, leaving Emmett and Zara standing in the foyer staring at each other. Emmett still had the ring box in his hand.

Even though he was seriously disappointed that his proposal wasn't going to happen as he'd planned it, he couldn't deny the surprised look on her face and how happy it made him. He started to chuckle. Leave it to kids to toss a big ol' wrench into best-laid plans.

So he did what he'd planned to do in roughly six hours. He dropped to one knee and held out the ring box. "Zara *Brilliant* Olsen, you call me on my bullshit, you challenge me to be a better man, you make me want to be a better man, and because of you, I think I am. You are the most incredible thing to have come into my life since my daughter, and I couldn't have asked for a better woman for her to call her *stepmom*. I would love it if you would agree to be my wife, my partner and my co-parent. Ring in every new year with me from now until forever."

"Why's my dad on his knee?" JoJo whispered behind him.

Emmett hadn't heard the children sneak back up on them. When they wanted to be quiet, they could be; otherwise, they were like a herd of buffalo wearing Christmas bells.

"I think this is how you ask someone to marry you. At least that's how I've seen it in the movies," Nolan whispered back. "Mom, you gonna say *yes*?" he asked, his voice no longer a whisper.

Emmett hadn't taken his eyes off Zara. Her sapphire-blue eyes had welled up with tears, and her cheeks held a beautiful pink flush. Her mouth, now pressed in a thin flat line, jiggled as she fought to keep her emotions in check, her nostrils flaring with the intensity of her struggle.

"Mom?" Nolan asked again. "What's your answer?"

"Yeah," Josie echoed, "what's your answer? Do I have a new big brother?"

Emmett's lip twitched. But at the same time, unease began to worm its way beneath his skin. Had she not answered because she was going to answer *no* and she wasn't sure how to do it in front of the kids? Or was she thinking it over?

A tear slipped down her rosy cheek, but she quickly wiped it away with the sleeve of her coat.

Emmett's knee was beginning to ache from being down on it on the cold tile for so long.

Would it be rude if he stood up and waited for her answer on his two feet?

Zara blinked, then finally nodded. "Yes, I will marry you."

For a few reasons, Emmett was up off his knee and wrapping his arms around the woman he loved in less than a nanosecond.

The kids whooped and hollered behind them. Then Emmett and Zara found themselves tackled at the waists by their children, hugging them.

"What took you so long, Mom?" Nolan asked, his arms still around them.

Zara snickered in Emmett's arms. Emmett chuckled too. Children were so impatient.

"Yeah?" JoJo asked. "I was getting tired of waiting."

That made three of them.

Zara's titter turned into a full-size laugh, and she tossed her head back, closed her eyes and opened her mouth. Emmett took the invitation—even if it wasn't one—and sealed his mouth over hers.

"Ewwww," the children said in unison, releasing their parents.

"That's gross. You both have germs, you know," JoJo said. "What if you get each other sick?"

"Come on, Josie," Nolan said, disgust in his tone. "You can help me make the pizzas. But *don't* touch the big knife." Once again, their voices disappeared around the corner into the kitchen.

Emmett slipped his tongue into Zara's mouth and held her tighter against him. She felt so good, so right in his arms. Her heart beating next to his was where it was meant to be, forever and always. He thanked every star in the sky when it was a clear night that she'd given him another chance two years ago. He had still been allowing his divorce from Tiff—his past—haunt his present and his future, and Zara helped him see that there was so much more joy left to experience in the world. And his life was all the richer to have a wonderful woman like her to share it all with.

Eventually, though, she broke their kiss and blinked up at him, her eyes still watery. "I'm sorry if I made you nervous with my hesitation," she said, her lips now puffy from their fervent kisses. "My answer had been *yes* from the very start. I just thought I needed to come up with some equally beautiful acceptance speech in response to your heartrending query."

He smiled down at the woman he loved, the woman who had stolen his heart, but instead of running off with it, she'd only made it grow, made it stronger, made it fuller. "All I need from you is a *yes*," he said. "Say you'll be mine so I can be yours. Let's make it legal. You and Nolan practically live here anyway. Let's make it all official."

A small smile tilted her lips. "How can I say no? Your yard is just so much bigger than mine. I can plant so many more flowers."

"So that's why you're marrying me, because I have a big *yard?*"

She nodded and pinched her lips together sassily. "Mhmm. I love a man with a big *yard.*"

He tightened his hold around her and dipped her. "Oh, baby, my *yard* is huge. I can't wait for you to get your hands on it. Make it *grow.*"

Her chuckle warmed him. She really did have a great

laugh. He'd fallen in love with her laugh at their very first meeting and continued to fall for it each and every time that soft, joyful sound filled a room.

"We can rent your townhouse, or you can sell it and buy out half of this place. I'm good with whatever you want to do, baby. I just want you and Nolan in mine and JoJo's life for good. I want the four of us to be a family."

"I want that too."

"You two done kissing yet?" Nolan called from the kitchen. "We have pizzas to make."

"Yeah, and banana splits, too," JoJo added.

Zara and Emmett both began to laugh, each of them rolling their eyes as they reluctantly parted.

He unzipped her coat and helped her slide out of it, hanging it up on the coat hook behind them.

"We'll be there in a sec," Emmett called down the hallway to the children. He retrieved the ring box from her right hand and pulled the ring free from its soft satin cushion. He brought his voice down so just Zara could hear him now. "We need to see if this thing fits." He picked up her left hand. "Are you going to take it as a bad sign if it doesn't fit?"

His fiancée didn't say anything, but the subtle lift of her eyebrow said she was considering it. With a sly grin, she angled her ring finger up a bit to give him greater access, and he made to slide on the ring with its rose gold band (because duh, roses) and intricate floral halo diamond design. A large diamond in the middle, and twenty-four smaller diamonds surrounding it.

He held his breath.

It fit perfectly.

He exhaled.

Phew.

"It's perfect," she whispered, lifting her eyes from the ring to his face. New tears made the bright blue glow. "And so was your proposal."

He rolled his eyes again. "Kids certainly have a way of making things interesting, don't they?" He released her hand and reached for the two grocery bags before taking her hand once again and leading them both into the kitchen.

"They certainly do," she confirmed. "Though I think we should move the clocks forward tonight and have a kid-free new year where we make our own memories and keep things *interesting*."

Emmett squeezed her hand and waggled his eyebrows up and down. "You got it. Though I really don't see either of them lasting past ten."

They entered the kitchen hand in hand to find their children happily making pizzas together.

Emmett's heart swelled.

This was his family.

His daughter was happy, well-adjusted, and her heart was safe and full.

And now his heart was the same.

He and Zara wandered over to stand in front of their children. He plopped the grocery bags on the counter, then brought her around and placed her back to his front, wrapping his arms around her waist. His chin fell to her shoulder. "I love watching these two," he murmured, planting a kiss to her neck.

She placed her hands over his. "Me too."

"You want more kids?" he asked, making sure his voice remained low enough that the pizza twins didn't hear him.

She craned her neck around to look at him, disbelief and amusement in her eyes. "I'm forty-six years old. My baby-carrying days are behind me. I'm happy with the two we have. I think it's time we talk about the ol' *snip snip*." She made a scissor-cutting motion with her fingers.

The two we have.

He grinned and squeezed her tighter against him. "Me too. The *two* we have are perfect. And I'll meet with the doc for a referral on Monday. Let's block those swimmers."

She was still glancing up at him, and he took the loving gaze in her eyes and her slightly parted lips as an invitation to once again take her mouth. He'd never grow tired of kissing his woman and would take every opportunity he could to do so.

"Not again," JoJo groaned. "They kiss a lot."

"Can you guys go do that somewhere else?" Nolan asked. "We're trying to make dinner here, and you two are just goofing around."

Emmett pulled his lips away from Zara's but left them hovering just above. "Can we go kiss in the living room?" he asked, glancing at the kids.

They both nodded.

Smiling, he spun Zara out of his arms and took her hand. "Do what you can for the pizzas. You've both helped us make them before. When you've gone as far as you can on your own, let us know, and we'll come help you finish." Then he led his wife-to-be off in the direction of the living room, lifting her up into his arms once they were around the corner and out of the children's view.

Zara giggled, looping her arms around his until they toppled to the couch, Emmett on top of her. "Those kids ... "

"Are wonderfully independent," he said with a growl, covering her body and kissing her neck. "Any chance we can send them to bed *now?*"

She laughed beneath him. "It's six o'clock, and they can both tell time. Afraid not."

He peppered kisses over her neck, cheeks, chin and finally landed back on her mouth. "Never hurts to ask."

She wrapped her arms around his neck and began to play

with the hair at the nape of his neck. "You're right, it doesn't. And I'm so glad you asked me to marry you."

Reaching behind him, he took her left hand and laced it with his, kissing the back of it before bringing the ring into view. "Michael and Shane helped me pick it out."

"They do have superb taste. Though you do too, and I'm sure I would have loved something you picked out as well." The twinkle in her eye said she was being generous with her compliment.

He kissed her ring finger. "Yeah, but you're also glad I asked for their opinion."

She grinned. "I am."

"You're going to have to call them with the news. They're waiting impatiently by their phone." Zara's best friend and his husband were so excited to help plan the wedding. Without even asking if Emmett was okay with it, they already planned to show up tomorrow with a stack of bridal magazines. Emmett planned to sleep in.

"I'll call them in a bit," she said, tugging on his hair with her free hand. "Right now, I'm going to make out with my fiancé." She angled her mouth beneath his. "Here's to a lifetime of friendship, purpose and unconditional love."

"And hot sex on wine barrels."

She slipped her tongue into his mouth but not before murmuring, "And hot sex on wine barrels."

Then he kissed the last woman he would ever kiss, and together they rang in the new year with their children and started to plan not only a wedding, but a true happily ever after.

VALENTINE'S WITH THE SINGLE DAD - SNEAK PEEK

SINGLE DADS OF SEATTLE BOOK 7

Chapter 1

She was back.

Same time.

Same table.

Same drink order.

Same little pink notebook and pen.

Only today, her hair was different. Normally, she kept her short, chin-length, dark brown bob straight with a soft swoosh over her forehead, but today she'd gone and let it get all wavy and had secured the swoosh with a little silver clip on the side of her head.

It helped him see her eyes better.

He really liked her eyes.

Bright gray with soft flecks of white around the iris. He'd never seen anybody with eyes like that before. And the way the corners crinkled when she smiled or took a sip of her wine, made the apples of her cheeks lift and go extra round.

He had no idea what her name was because she kept to

herself, but for the past three weeks the woman had been coming into his bar every Tuesday and Thursday night. She would sit in the same spot, every night. Order the same thing, every night. And there she would stay from eight fifteen until ten fifteen. She would drink nothing but wine or water, and over the course of those two hours she would entertain— though it looked more like interview—a different man every half-hour or so. Some men made it th nearly the one-hour mark. While others were sent on their way before their drinks turned warm.

They would chat, she would smile, but ultimately let him do the majority of the talking. Then, they would shake hands and the man would be on his way—never to return again, or so it seemed.

Was she doing her own variation of speed dating?

Was she interviewing them for jobs?

Was she a pimp—or a madam and vetting potential gigolos?

All the guys who had sat down with her so far were not trolls, in fact, they were all pretty decent looking, so maybe she was interviewing them for an all-male burlesque show.

Either way, the woman who sat at the table by the window intrigued the crap out of Mason. He thought about her all the time. She was like a song or tune stuck in his head. He just couldn't shake her—and he didn't want to.

He looked forward to Tuesday and Thursday nights. He'd actually switched his shifts around with the general manager so that he always worked Tuesday and Thursday nights. This mystery woman had put a spell on him, and he just needed to know more.

What was her name?

Where did she work?

What was she doing every Tuesday and Thursday night, sitting in his bar with a different man every thirty minutes?

Normally, he would have had no problem walking up to the woman, offering her his hand and asking what she was up to. He was, after all, the owner of Prime Sports Bar and Grill, and a very friendly, outgoing person, but for some reason, he got the sense that she wanted to be left alone and to her own devices. She had a slight sense of almost embarrassment in her face as she met each man, shook his hand and sat down with him. As if she didn't really want to be there, but was doing so because she had to. It only made the mystery behind her all the more alluring, all the more exciting.

She was also crazy-cute, and for the first time in a very long time, he felt butterflies in his stomach at the thought of approaching her for more than just her drink order.

He glanced at his watch—it was closing in on ten o'clock. She would be leaving soon.

Pulling the lever on the tap for the San Camanez Lager, he filled up a pint for an order that had just come in. He'd gotten so good at filling up a draft that he didn't really have to pay attention, or watch what he was doing. He simply counted in his head, tilted the glass just right and ninety-nine percent of the time he was dead on when he dropped his gaze again and pulled the pint glass free.

Tonight was in that ninety-nine percent.

He plopped the beer stein down onto the bar so the waitress could come and grab it along with the rest of the drinks ordered. His eyes remained glued to the back of the man's head who was currently entertaining—or should he say failing to entertain—Mason's mystery woman.

Then the guy stood up.

Mason glanced at his watch again. Oh, this guy was obviously a dud, he didn't even make the full thirty minutes.

The dud grabbed his coat off the back of his chair and slipped his arms into the sleeves before nodding at Mason's mystery woman and then making haste to leave the bar, leaving her sitting there all alone, a bored, disappointed look on her face.

Was she going to get up and leave now?

She never stayed past ten-fifteen and it was now ten o'clock, surely, she didn't have another "date" lined up.

He hoped she didn't.

He checked in with his mother to see how his four-month daughter Willow was doing. She'd had a bit of a cold last week and was still a touch congested, but seemed to be sleeping better and in brighter spirits. His mother claimed that all was well with Willow, and that she'd fallen asleep on Mason's father's chest, and even though Willow could sleep in her bassinet, Mason's dad hadn't bothered to move her.

"They're only little for such a short time," his mother had said. "Let us indulge in her babyness for as long as we can."

Mason simply rolled his eyes. Who was he to get upset when he did the same thing? Whenever Willow fell asleep on his chest, the world stopped and he simply took in the moment. His mother was right, they were only little for such a short time. Before he knew it, she would be crawling, and then walking, and then out with her friends with no time for dear old dad.

His heart ached at the thought of his little Willow old enough to go to parties and spend time with boys. Was it too late to have a tracking device implanted behind her ear?

Slowly, as the minutes ticked by, the bar began to empty, but his mystery woman remained. All the servers left, and the kitchen closed in ten minutes. All who lingered was just a couple of women in their mid-forties chatting away near the back of the pub, and Mason's mystery woman.

She was staring at her notebook, but he could tell by the way she tapped her pen on the paper and chewed on her bottom lip that she wasn't really paying attention to whatever she'd written. She was lost in thought.

Mason needed to let her know it was last call. They closed at eleven on Tuesdays.

He dried his hand on a towel and stepped out from behind the bar. Tossing his shoulders back and cracking his neck side to side, he approached her table. "Hey there, it's last call, would you like another pinot?" He stopped directly in front of her and waited for her to lift her head, her eyes slowly climbing his body. He resisted the urge to grin, even though he secretly got a big thrill when her gray eyes widen as they fell to the front of his pants.

Her throat bobbed on a swallow when her gaze finally landed on his face. She blinked. "Yes, please," she said softly, her eyes drifting back down to her notepad.

"Are you meeting anybody else tonight?" He couldn't stop himself. The curiosity was like an itch he just needed to scratch.

Slowly, she shook her head but didn't lift her eyes back up to him. "No, I'm not."

Mason swallowed and teetered on his heels. "Can I ask what you've been up to all these weeks? You're here twice a week for two hours meeting with several different men an evening." He scratched the back of his neck. "The waitresses are starting to talk."

That wasn't a lie. The servers were starting to question what this woman's angle was, but Mason doubted their curiosity was as strong as his, otherwise, they could have asked her.

Once again, her gaze climbed him. "I'm trying to hire a date," she said, her cheeks turning a beautiful shade of pink. "I hiring a date for a wedding."

Mason's bottom lip dropped. That hadn't been the answer

he'd been expecting at all. Why in the world did this gorgeous creature need to pay somebody to date her? He could only imagine that any red-blooded man in his right mind would jump at the chance to take her out her for free.

He needed to know more. He needed to know the full story.

"You hungry?" he asked.

She squinted at him, but then nodded. He could just see the cogs spinning in her brain as she tried to figure out what he was up to.

He wasn't even sure what he was up to yet, all he knew was that he wasn't ready to watch her walk out the door, and now that he's started talking to her, he needed to continue. He needed to get to know her.

"Gonna see if Barry in the back can make me a plate of nachos before the kitchen closes. Wanna share? On the house if you tell me the full story of why you feel the need to pay for a date."

This woman was very cautious. The way she stewed on his words, and took a serious pause before replying had him wondering if he'd come on too strong and she was suddenly going to grab her purse and dash out, never to return.

But that wasn't the case.

Thankfully.

Her head bobbed and she stood up, grabbing her coat and purse from the back of her chair, and then finally that little pink notebook and pen. "I'll join you at the bar," she said, standing up to her full height, which was a hell of a lot shorter than him. He hadn't realized just how short she was. He'd always approached her when she was sitting down.

Nodding and resisting the urge to fist pump in the air, he grabbed her empty wine glass off the table, as well as the half-finished beer of her last potential date-for-hire, and then headed back behind the bar.

He quickly poured her a glass of the pinot she'd been drinking every night for the past few weeks then slid the glass across the shiny wooden bar. "All right, Ms ..."

"Lowenna Chambers," she said, accepting the glass and immediately taking a sip.

Lowenna Chambers.

He rolled her name around on his tongue for a moment. He liked it. It suited her. It held a sense of sophistication he'd picked up the first night she'd come in.

"And your name?" she asked, her head tilted to the side, waiting.

He paused what he was doing and thrust his hand forward. "Mason Whitfield. Pleased to meet you, Ms. Chambers."

Her smiled warmed his chest from the center outward as she took his hand and shook it with a strength he felt all the way down to his balls. "Pleased to meet you too, Mr. Whitfield."

With a grin, he began to punch in their nacho order on the computer screen in front of him. "All right, Ms. Chambers, do you like jalapeños on your nachos?"

Her smile was small and almost coy, but she nodded. "I do."

"What about olives?"

She nodded again, her grin growing wider. "The more the better."

His smile also grew. "My kind of woman. Me too." He hit the extra olives button a few times to emphasize their obsession. "And guac?"

"Is it nachos without?"

Oh, he liked her. She'd been a bit timid at first when he approached her, but now she seemed to be a bit more comfortable with him, more relaxed.

"Absolutely not," he agreed. "I'll order us an extra large

guac." He hit the button to send it off to the kitchen, then went to work putting the stack of dirty glasses through the cleaner. "Okay, nachos are on their way. Now let's talk about his date-for-hire thing. Why in the world do you need to pay for a date?"

She took another sip of her wine before answering. "The long of the short of it is, my sister is marrying my ex-husband and I need a date to their wedding who will upstage them and their pompous, ostentatious, pretentious affair in every which way. I need a show stopper. I need an underwear model with an ivy league education, a six-figure salary who dances like Fred Astaire."

Whoa!

She lifted one shoulder. "You know ... a unicorn."

Mason had two glasses in each hand, one of them slippery and he nearly dropped it. "Um, can't you just ask the guy to say he's all those things?" Wouldn't that be easier than hunting for the holy grail and then paying the man to be her date? Surely there was a man out there who fit the bill for at least a few of those things and then they could fudge the rest.

She shook her head. "I don't want to lie. Lies always have a way of coming back to bite us in the ass. And if for whatever reason he forgets who is he's supposed to be that'll ruin everything."

Fair enough.

"So you're vetting dates in my bar then?" He resumed putting the glasses on the rotating cleaner.

"Seemed like a safe place to do it. Out in public, and you seem like a man who would jump to my defense if the guy I was interviewing got belligerent."

Oh, most definitely.

"So you picked my bar because I'm a free bodyguard?" He cocked an eyebrow but couldn't stop the smile that crooked his lips.

"I'm spending an awful lot of money on wine each week, I wouldn't call it free," she countered.

Fair enough.

"So, I get that it's a sore spot that your sister is marrying your ex-husband, but why not just boycott the wedding entirely? Why even put yourself through all of this and go in the first place?"

She exhaled out a deep breath. "Five years ago, I was diagnosed with uterine cancer. I had to have a full hysterectomy, because once they got in there, they found out the cancer had spread to my ovaries and a few other organs as well. My husband, Brody, was a first-year law associate at the time. His benefits were good, but not great. They covered a fair bit, but things still became tight and we struggled financially. My treatments and surgery were not cheap and the insurance company did everything they could do to deny us coverage."

Something began to tingle at the base of his neck but he couldn't put his finger on it just yet. "Motherfuckers," he grumbled, shaking his head.

"Agreed," she said with near tangible venom in her tone. "Anyway, Brody and my sister Doneen started sleeping together shortly after my surgery, once I started chemo. I was too sick to even think about being intimate and was also in recovery after major surgery."

"You're fucking kidding me?" This time he actually did drop a glass, the sound of it smashing to the tile floor startling both of them. His bottom lip dropped open again.

She shook her head completely unaffected by the shattered glass. "Nope. They don't know that I know, but I do. Brody filed for divorce once it was declared I was cancer free. He stated that although he still loved me, he was no longer in love with me. He also wanted to be a father and have children the traditional way. He just wasn't sure I was the woman for him anymore. Three months after he filed for divorce, he and Doneen made their relationship public."

Mason was busy sweeping up the glass, his knuckles white around the dustpan handle as he swept the shards into a pile. Rage pumped hot through him at the thought of this Brody douche and Lowenna's sister sneaking behind her back all while she was fighting for her life.

He dumped the glass into the trash bin then turned to face her in utter disbelief. "And you're going to their wedding?"

She nodded, her smile stiff. "Oh, there's more."

What else could there possibly be?

"I own a chocolate shop and they've asked me to make them a big, gaudy chocolate feature for the dessert table, along with all the favors for each guest at their place setting —for free of course. As a wedding gift. Doneen also asked me to be her maid of honor, but I was forced to decline as I said I couldn't do both her bridal shower, bachelorette party and all the chocolates for the wedding. I made her choose, and she said the chocolates were more important."

"Is your sister a psychopath?" he asked, completely serious in his question.

Her lip twitched. "More like socially unaware, completely self-absorbed and a vapid narcissist. I'm not sure she has any empathy either." She paused for a moment then shrugged. "Maybe she is a psychopath. I have heard more of them walk among us than we realize. Not all of them are machete-wielding lunatics."

Oh, he knew that well. He'd met a fair few psychopaths in his day. Most of them high-powered CEOs that had zero qualms destroying lives, businesses and entire communities if it lined their pockets with more cold, hard cash.

The bell in the kitchen dinged and he stepped around the corner to the food window to grab their nachos.

Lowenna's eyes went wide as he plopped the big tray down on the bar in front of her, the top a delicious, steaming blend of cheddar cheese and black olives. His mouth watered.

"So you run a chocolate shop?" he asked, handing her a plate and a few napkins. "Not that new chocolate place around the corner?"

"Wicked Sister Chocolates? Yep, that's me." Her grin was just that—wicked. "Bit of an ironic name, which is why I picked it. Doneen told me, when I was in the middle of my chemo treatment, losing my hair and no more than a hundred pounds, that I was making everything all about me. She told me that I brought cancer into our family and that I was all our parents ever talked about. That they forgot her birthday because they were at the hospital with me after I had a bad reaction to the chemo. She said I was wickedly selfish and milking my illness, that women got uterine cancer all the time and lived through it. That I was clearly making it out to be worse than it really was."

"What the ever-loving fuck?" Mason blurted out, a chip loaded with guac and salsa falling from his hand onto his shoe. "What. The. Fuck?"

All Lowenna did was her lift her eyebrows. "Yep. That's dear ol' sis for you. Nicest big sister I ever could have asked for."

"And you're going to her wedding?"

She shrugged again. "She's my sister."

"And she's a fucking psychopath who started sleeping with your husband while you were still married to him and battling cancer." He shook his head. He just couldn't wrap his brain around why Lowenna hadn't cut her sister out of her life with a broadsword.

And then impaled her with that sword.

If that had been Mason, he would no longer have a

sibling, he would sever all ties and live his life as an only child.

Thank God his sister, Nova, had the biggest heart in the world and was one of his best friends. It just sucked that she and her husband had moved to Australia last year for her husband's job. He missed her madly.

"I'm going because I need to show them that I've moved on. Because I have. I'm cancer free and business is booming. My life is really good right now. But I just feel like a show-stopper of a date, one infinitely hotter than my ex will help boost my confidence. Something that I've been lacking since you know ... my husband left me for my sister and all." She shoved a chip heaped with guac into her mouth, chewed, swallowed and then continued. "I have already booked dance lessons if he looks like Channing Tatum but doesn't dance like him. If he doesn't own a suit, I will rent him one. I will pay for his haircut. I will foot the bill for everything so long as he pretends to be madly in love with me and wins over every person at that party."

"But you said you want him to look like an underwear model and have a six-figure job, so he can probably afford all of that himself?"

She shrugged, then dipped a chip into the salsa. "Perhaps. I just need him to be more successful than my ex-husband and more handsome. What he does is irrelevant." Her eyes slid sideways. "Well, not irrelevant. Brody and Doneen are judgmental jerks, so as much as I would have no problem dating a garbage man, they'd laugh their asses off if they found out that's what he did. Even if he owned the entire waste management company, they wouldn't care and they'd look down their noses at him."

"When's the wedding?" he asked.

"My birthday," she said with a snort.

He cocked his head, and hit her with a probing gaze. "Which is?"

She drained her wine glass and then snorted again. "Valentine's Day."

IF YOU'VE ENJOYED THIS BOOK

If you've enjoyed this book, please consider leaving a review.
It really does make a difference.
Thank you again.
Xoxo
Whitley Cox

ACKNOWLEDGMENTS

There are so many people to thank who help along the way. Publishing a book is definitely not a solo mission, that's for sure. First and foremost, my friend and editor Chris Kridler, you lady are a blessing, a gem and an all-around amazing human being. Thank you for your honesty and hard work.

Thank you, to my critique groups gals, Danielle and Jillian. I love our meetups where we give honest feedback and just bitch about life. You two are my bitch-sisters and I wouldn't give you up for anything.

Andi Babcock for her beta-read, I always appreciate your attention to detail and comments.

Author Jeanne St. James, my alpha reader and sister from another mister, what would I do without you?

Megan J. Parker-Squiers from EmCat Designs, your covers are awesome. Thank you,

My Naughty Room Readers Crew, authors Jeanne St. James, Erica Lynn and Cailin Briste, I love being part of such a tremendous set of inspiring, talented and supportive women. Thank you for letting me learn, lean on and join the team.

My street team, Whitley Cox's Curiously Kinky Reviewers, you are all awesome and I feel so blessed to have found such wonderful fans.

The ladies in Vancouver Island Romance Authors, your support and insight have been incredibly helpful, and I'm so honored to be a part of a group of such talented writers.

Author Cora Seton for your help, tweaks and suggestions for my blurbs, as always, they come back from you so sparkly. I also love our walks, talks and heart-to-hearts, they mean so much to me.

Authors Kathleen Lawless, Nancy Warren and Jane Wallace, I love our writing meetups. Wine, good food and friendship always make the words flow.

My parents, in-laws and brother, thank you for your unwavering support.

The Small Human and the Tiny Human, you are the beats and beasts of my heart, the reason I breathe and the reason I drink. I love you both to infinity and beyond.

And lastly, of course, the husband. You are my forever. I love you.

ALSO BY WHITLEY COX

Quick & Dirty

Book 1, A Quick Billionaires Novel

Quick & Easy

Book 2, A Quick Billionaires Novella

Quick & Reckless

Book 3, A Quick Billionaires Novel

Hot Dad

Lust Abroad

Snowed In & Set Up

Quick & Dangerous

Book 4, A Quick Billionaires Novel

Hired by the Single Dad

The Single Dads of Seattle, Book 1

Dancing with the Single Dad

The Single Dads of Seattle, Book 2

Saved by the Single Dad

The Single Dads of Seattle, Book 3

Living with the Single Dad

The Single Dads of Seattle, Book 4

Christmas with the Single Dad

The Single Dads of Seattle, Book 5

New Years with the Single Dad

The Single Dads of Seattle, Book 6

Upcoming

Valentine's with the Single Dad

The Single Dads of Seattle, Book 7

Neighbors with the Single Dad

The Single Dads of Seattle, Book 8

Flirting with the Single Dad

The Single Dads of Seattle, Book 9

Falling for the Single Dad

The Single Dads of Seattle, Book 10

Lost Hart

The Harty Boys Book 2

ABOUT THE AUTHOR

A Canadian West Coast baby born and raised, Whitley is married to her high school sweetheart, and together they have two beautiful daughters and a fluffy dog. She spends her days making food that gets thrown on the floor, vacuuming Cheerios out from under the couch and making sure that the dog food doesn't end up in the air conditioner. But when nap time comes, and it's not quite wine o'clock, Whitley sits down, avoids the pile of laundry on the couch, and writes.

A lover of all things decadent; wine, cheese, chocolate and spicy erotic romance, Whitley brings the humorous side of sex, the ridiculous side of relationships and the suspense of everyday life into her stories. With mommy wars, body issues, threesomes, bondage and role playing, these books have everything we need to satisfy the curious kink in all of us.

YOU CAN ALSO FIND ME HERE

Website: WhitleyCox.com
Twitter: @WhitleyCoxBooks
Instagram: @CoxWhitley
Facebook Page: https://www.facebook.com/CoxWhitley/
Blog: https://whitleycox.blogspot.ca/
Multi-Author Blog: https://romancewritersbehavingbadly.blogspot.com
Exclusive Facebook Reader Group: https://www.facebook.com/groups/234716323653592/
Booksprout: https://booksprout.co/author/994/whitley-cox
Bookbub: https://www.bookbub.com/authors/whitley-cox

JOIN MY STREET TEAM

DON'T FORGET TO SUBSCRIBE TO MY NEWSLETTER

Be the first to hear about pre-orders, new releases, giveaways, 99 cent deals, and freebies!

Click here to Subscribe
http://eepurl.com/ckh5yT

Made in the USA
Las Vegas, NV
08 September 2021

29870800R00125